ARNA

THE JOURNAL OF THE

UNIVERSITY OF SYDNEY ARTS STUDENTS SOCIETY

2012

First published 2012 by Darlington Press
Funded by The University of Sydney Union
and The University of Sydney Faculty of Arts

ISBN 978-1-921364-26-6

Fisher Library F03
University of Sydney
NSW 2006 Australia
Email: sup.info@sydney.edu.au
Web: sydney.edu.au/sup

Cover photo by Eleanor Gibson

In memory of
Robert Studley Forrest Hughes
(1938–2012)
Rest in peace

ARNA is brought to you by

Editors-in-Chief	Alex McKinnon
	Eleanor Gordon-Smith
General Editors	Nicholas Simone
	Gemma Davies
Creative Editors	Gabriella Edelstein
	Bryant Apolonio
	Madeleine Watts
Poetry Editors	Claire Nashar
	Alberta Mackenzie
	Darren Lesaguis
Visual Arts Editors	Flora Grant
	Richard Gao
	Crisia Miriou
Critical Editors	Matthew Clarke
	Rachel Bailes
	Astha Rajvanshi
Designer	Rafi Alam

Thanks to

The University of Sydney Union
The University of Sydney Faculty of Arts
The Sydney Arts Student Society
Mike de Waal
Agata Mrva-Montoya
Mungo MacCallum
Les Murray
Contributors
You, for buying

Contents

Foreword

Mungo MacCallum

Long, long ago, when computers were young and huge and Bob
Menzies had been in power for a mere generation, I was an Arts
student at Sydney University.

I had many prominent and congenial contemporaries—Clive
James, Les Murray, John Bell, Bob Ellis—the list went on seemingly
indefinitely. But unknown to us, lurking in the Law School on
Macquarie Street, was another, more sinister presence: John
Winston Howard.

In due course we all graduated, and while my friends and I
spread out, rejoicing, across the world Howard retreated to the
bosom of his family and began plotting the destruction of the
system that had produced us.

Little Johnny may never have heard Hermann Goering's famous
(and possibly apocryphal) dictum: 'When I hear the word culture, I
reach for my revolver,' but he took a similarly jack-booted approach
to the subject.

The Arts were something strange and alien: the Other. So when
he eventually achieved greatness (or, rather, had it thrust upon
him) the Arts ranked high on his paranoiac schedule of real and
imagined enemies to be destroyed. And so did the trade union
movement: it appeared that he had been frightened by a unionist in
his infancy. And where were these two horrors to be Why, back at
that place he had escaped back in 1961 to go home to mother, the
university.

It has been claimed that the Howard government's onslaught
against compulsory student unionism was based on a semantic
confusion: that he actually believed that student unions were a
similar construct to their workplace counterparts. Certainly he
used the comparison to convince his thicker colleagues to support

his campaign, but he himself knew better: after all, he had been there, at least peripherally.

Howard's target was not the union as such, but the freewheeling, open, liberal lifestyle it supported. This was the environment that encouraged a defiance of convention, a rejection of community (well, his) values, internationalism, rebellion—and unforgivably, its political orientation was, not infrequently, towards the left. It had be extirpated, razed from the face of the earth. And the abolition of compulsory student unionism would starve it to death.

The National Party pleaded that an exception be made in the case of sport (though not, presumably, rugby union). But apart from that, it was blitzkrieg—take no prisoners. The incomprehensible and probably pornographic poets, the effete, dress-up theatricals, the whole snooty-tooty, arty-farty bunch were to be exterminated.

But somehow there were survivors, clawing themselves from the ruins of what were once independent, welcoming places to learn about life in all its glorious complexity but now resembled conveyor belts with a cash register at one end and at the other a piece of paper which doubled as a receipt and proof that you had survived the passage. In places, at first isolated, but slowly fighting their way back from the darkness, the flames still flickered – still flicker, giving the hope and promise that one day they may burst back into a cleansing fire that will consume all traces of the dark years of Howard.

And one of these flames is ARNA—a reminder of the Sydney University my friends and I enjoyed all those years ago. Long may it glow and brightly may it burn.

It May Just Come True

David Schuman

He didn't know what to do with her blank stare. It infuriated him. Tanner F. Murray rarely felt like he didn't control the situation. By his estimates, the last time was when Jessica Kaplan rejected him at the seventh grade Valentine's Day dance. She didn't want to be his girlfriend. She still had a thing for the Reverend's kid. He had had a leather jacket.

It had generally been easy for Tanner. Some would say too easy. But the bar smelled kind of funky that night. It seemed the puke odour was making its way out of the men's room stall. That didn't explain why she was giving him such a blank stare though. He tried again. 'So how are you finding classes so far?' She hadn't bitten on the standard introductory conversation routine of 'where-you-from-who-you-know.'

Her straight blonde hair brushed to the side when she shrugged her shoulders. Tanner couldn't tell if the half-smile she cracked signified disinterest. It must be though because she just wasn't talking. Her mouth opened—yes, finally! It closed again. Tanner tried to keep smiling. He was shifting his weight back and forth now. Left ... right ... left.

'What are you taking?' She recited her list. Econ., calculus. It didn't matter. There was one thing he could do that may spark up some conversation. 'Do you want a drink? What do you want?' Alcohol could be an interesting topic. Maybe tease her about her fondness for cosmopolitans while disclosing in a hushed voice that he himself had a weakness for the colorful libations. And tell her if it were socially acceptable, he'd be holding a vodka cranberry as they spoke. Make sure to keep that playful smile on.

At the least, another drink might get her to open up a bit. Was she actually just staring at the wall while he waited at the bar? This was becoming unbearable. Girls were all over the place. But an inexplicable urge to fight past the lack of chemistry was lodged inside him. There was absolutely no reason to still be standing there with her, but he abhorred the feeling of a wasted half-hour on a Thursday night. The mindless trash heap of conversation continued to pile up. Tanner's frustration was actually beginning to subside into boredom. He still couldn't leave though. It bothered him that despite his boredom, his loafers still seemed to be cemented to the floor.

He realised what was happening. She was a conversational black hole. Where all the small talk in the world goes to die. A conundrum because Tanner was so good at it. He could small-talk them all the way back to the bedroom. She was a freshman too. She was cake. Or she should be.

After the drinks were done and his last question had been lost to her abyss, Tanner made up his mind. He couldn't do this. After tonight, if he ever saw her, his eyes would merely traipse past her. Move along, nothing to see here. And she would wonder fruitlessly why that boy who spent so much time with her that one night never noticed her again. She would furrow her brow and decide not to tell her friends.

'Rebecca, do you want to get out of here?' Without any hint of a torch being lit behind her eyes, Rebecca raised her eyebrows ever so slightly. Then she nodded. 'Okay.' Tanner threw on his good-guy smile, let his gaze linger, and turned toward the door. Once his back was to her, the smile was gone. He rolled his eyes. He sensed the looks of his buddies, their electromagnetic waves of approval honing in on him from every corner of the place like he was a magnet. It didn't give Tanner the usual feeling this time. She was a knockout, no one would argue that, but he really didn't like her. Yes, he had gone from being frustrated to being bored to despising her. No person is good enough to be that bad at holding a conversation.

He hoped she was following him. As he stood on the sidewalk trying to hail a cab, he couldn't meet her big blue eyes. Maybe she was one of those girls that never got happy about anything, but never said 'no' either. You would always be unsure of what she was really thinking but what did it matter? She was going along with what he wanted. It inspired a loose confidence in him as they rode along in the cab. He could do no wrong despite the distinct feeling he wasn't doing anything right.

Rebecca might have mentioned something about living with three other girls. They went upstairs and as he was holding her bedroom door open like a true Southern gent, Tanner realised he was going to sleep with her. He slowly closed the door behind him, careful not to wake any potential housemates, and glanced at her bedside clock: 1:47.

She was sitting on the edge of her pink comforter with her hands in her lap. She was smiling, no mistake about that. The staring again made Tanner a little antsy. He was walking over to her, trying to feign interest, when she said, 'Wait, Tanner. Turn the lights off.' That was something he did not see coming. Nevertheless, he obeyed.

When he had groped his way back over to the bed and sat down, Rebecca pounced. She clutched his shoulders with a strength he didn't expect from a girl her size. Tanner felt wet lips press against his and her knee swung over his groin so she was straddling him. The dance had started. It was the aggression that hooked him. All at once, she opened up her legs and simultaneously opened him to his core. The pounding in his chest almost drowned out the intoxicating noises ejecting from her mouth. Her nails were going back and forth from digging valleys into his chest to her own scalp. The girl from the bar had disappeared and Tanner no longer recognized this creature on top of him.

His bulging eyes were glued to the ceiling afterward. The only memento Tanner ever kept of a girl was a singular lasting image. It could be their smile or it could be their disappointment when he had hurt their feelings. It might be the view he had looking down on them in bed, a face hidden in shadow. Maybe it was the way they fell into a slouch when he inevitably broke off the relationship. He had amassed a sizable collection of these snapshots, each one a souvenir from his career as a red-blooded male. On this Thursday night though, Rebecca de Corday hijacked all of these memories and carelessly set them aflame, leaving herself as the only girl that that mattered anymore in Tanner's life.

He got ready to leave the next morning, but unlike last night, he now really tried to force some good conversation. Her response could be generously described as extreme disinterest. After the sexual performance she had put on, this alarmed him. In fact, it threw him off for the whole week. Tanner couldn't exactly put his finger on it, but a gloom had descended. The thought of the weekend didn't perk him up like it usually did. Glances from the passing beautiful girls didn't quicken his heart rate. Murph's tales of conquest and Smitty's feats of alcohol consumption just weren't as entertaining. Boat shoe leather didn't hold the same shine. It was all Rebecca. She had driven his carefree collegian's life to an abrupt halt. He couldn't stop thinking about her.

On Wednesday, Tanner saw her walking across campus with a guy that he assumed was another freshman. It was chilly, and Rebecca looked adorable all bundled up. Stylish, too. She had curled her blonde hair. Tanner approached the two of them with all the confidence befitting a junior fraternity man.

'Rebecca, hey, what's going on?' Tanner kept pace with the two of them. Not a speck of attention was wasted on the other guy.

'Oh, hi.'

'Hey, what are you doing tomorrow night? My friends and I are thinking of going downtown.'

'That sounds fun.'

'Yeah, it should be. I'll text you. See you. Um. Later.' Tanner's voice trailed off as he let them walk ahead. Why wouldn't she talk to him? He had been on his way to meet Smitty for lunch in the dining hall. The burgers tasted like cardboard. All around him,

Tanner heard the clamour of the the the cafeteria. Girls and guys, everyone enjoying each other's company. He didn't know what to think when an urge to have all that with Rebecca de Corday arose in him.

Tanner texted her the next night. No response. This helplessness was foreign and uncomfortable. He believed in talking things out, but he knew he was beginning to repeat himself around his friends about this girl Rebecca who was great in bed, but either had no interest in Tanner or just lacked all social ability. Her black hole had sucked in more than just his efforts at conversation though: even he couldn't understand his own infatuation with her. His inner dialogue kept grasping emptily at justifications. With such an animalistic sexuality, there had to be more to her, but he couldn't figure out how to bring it out of her. If she really wasn't interested in him, well ... that thought just intensified his dejection.

Friday night, the Jack Daniels flowed freely while the Coke was nowhere to be found. Tanner's fortunes on this cloudless evening ended up in Melanie Dashwinder's hands, a girl who had been a favourite retread of his since February of freshman year. She was altogether crazy. Like a recently used Slinky, Melanie was always bouncing up and down ever so slightly. Tanner was pretty sure she had a mild lazy eye, but you could only notice it sometimes in pictures. Cute though. As soon as he stumbled over to her, she turned away from the guy she had been talking to. Her hand leapt to his shoulder and her teeth emerged. Her brown eyes gave away the fact that she had been drinking as well. They found a cab soon after.

The cloud that had been shadowing Tanner all week descended on him when he was opening his bedroom door. He was bored. Melanie was perky though so he had to put on a mask of a frat boy loving life. It had never been a mask before. The fooling around got more serious but Tanner just wanted her to leave. He slipped the condom on anyway and as he began the monotonous thrusting, he thought of what Smitty would say when he found out Melanie was sharing his bed yet again. He thought of what all the guys would say. And that somehow led to hearing his high school lacrosse coach. 'It is a privilege to play this game, not a right. You guys are just going through the motions! With effort like that, there's no way you'll ever be able to compete in this league.' The team had responded. They agreed later that the speech coach gave on that late March day was a turning point that helped them roll to a league championship. Thinking of it made Tanner want to roll off of Melanie.

He forced himself to look into her eyes. They were sharp, blue, piercing. Tanner blinked, and they were brown again. Twenty minutes later, Melanie was gone and Tanner was left alone, feeling hollow and drunk. He wanted Rebecca right then and now. He stiffened just at the thought of that night with her. In what he knew was a desperate last-ditch effort, Tanner reached over to his phone and punched out a text message. Miraculously, she agreed to come over.

Half an hour later, he went down to get her from the lobby of his building, wearing athletic pants and a T-shirt. She looked amazing in her heels, short black cocktail dress and just too much makeup.

'I'm glad you could come, Rebecca. You look great. What did you do tonight?' Tanner found it odd when she said she hadn't gone out. They didn't speak in the elevator ride up and Tanner felt a similar vibe to when he saw her walking the other day. But none of that mattered. She was here now, and he could feel himself beaming.

He opened his door for her, and as soon as they were both inside, she smiled seductively and squinted her eyes a little. Her pointer finger extended out to him and she said, 'Get over here.' She was suddenly dripping with confidence, as was he. He walked over to her with a smirk on his face and she pushed him down onto the bed. Another romp with Rebecca became another mind-blowing experience. She had to like him at least a little, right? He wanted to wrap his arms around her. He wanted everything about her.

Just like last time, she immediately fell asleep. No pillow talk. No snuggling. Tanner was glad Rebecca was here, but she was violating the usual female protocol. He drifted off as the tendrils of doubt began to curl around him once again.

Tanner woke up first. When he got back from brushing his teeth, he found Rebecca gathering her clothes.

'Good morning! How are you feeling on this fine day?' He tried to be peppy.

'Okay.' She was putting her shoes on and didn't look up.

'What do you want to do?'

'I'm going to go home.'

He offered to drive her, but she refused. He suggested getting food, but she said no. The conversation went on like this. It was all one-word answers. She didn't want to talk or laugh at any of his dumb jokes. She acted like she was in a hurry. He tried to kiss her as she was leaving, but she turned and he landed on her cheek. Tanner climbed back into bed, deflated. He meticulously dissected everything he had done. It was still baffling why she was so unresponsive. Nevertheless, Rebecca came over again the next weekend after another late text from Tanner. The next weekend too. She was proving to be incapable of any normal social interaction with him, but if anything, Tanner F. Murray was persistent.

She stopped sleeping over eventually. The post-coital emotional cocktail of self-doubt and frustration never went down easily for Tanner. One night as Rebecca was getting dressed to leave, Tanner got in the mood for some Melanie Dashwinder and that bubbly personality of hers. Just to change it up a little. He chuckled to himself mirthlessly. Tanner couldn't help but notice how good Rebecca looked. Then she left.

A few nights later, they saw each other before midnight for the first time in three weeks. They were in the bar where they first met. At the sight of her, Tanner's emotions boiled to the surface. The roller coaster had to end. With all the determination he could muster, Tanner left his friends and stormed over to her. She looked up with no expression.

'Can I talk to you for a minute? Outside?'

Tanner strode towards the entrance angrily. He waved his hand dismissively when the boys noticed Rebecca and started catcalling. The brisk air was a stinging slap but his irritation kept his cheeks nice and warm, as did the rum in his belly.

'Okay, listen. I need to know what's going on here with us. No, just let me talk. You pretty much won't even talk to me but you still come over all the time. And that's great, I love that part, but then you become this completely different person afterwards and it's driving me crazy. I don't know what to think. You just act so weird all the time and then you come over and I—I don't know.'

There was a pause. 'Tanner. I like you, I do, but what more do you want? We're just having a good time, I thought.'

Tanner realised he sounded crazy. She was right. He had a great situation going. 'We are having a good time, but, well, I can't get you out of my head. I think, uh, I think I like you. And I guess that means that you coming over and leaving isn't enough. It's not what I want.'

For the first time since he had known her, she gave him a genuine smile. Not seductive, not forced. She just looked happy. 'Really? Okay then.'

'Okay what?'

'Okay, then I'll do more than just come over. We can do other stuff too.'

Relief washed over Tanner, accompanied by amazement. 'Wow, great. Awesome.' He was finally able to don his cool-guy smirk again. 'So, this would be a pretty good time to get out of here, huh?'

Rebecca smiled at him again and said, 'Yes, I suppose it would be.' He could get used to that smile. They hailed a cab and Tanner was about to climb in after her when Melanie Dashwinder and four of her friends exited the bar behind him. He looked at them, and suddenly panicked. He saw two of Melanie's attractive friends he had always wanted to get to know better, and what about Melanie? They had been hooking up for almost two years.

He turned to Rebecca, who was waiting patiently for him. 'Is everything okay, Tanner?'

'Uh, yeah.' It was his turn to force a smile as he sat down. Rebecca immediately linked her arm through his and leaned her head against him. The driver pulled away and Tanner twisted around to see out the back window.

There they were. Melanie and her friends, laughing, flirting. They got smaller and smaller, until they couldn't be seen anymore. Then Tanner and Rebecca were alone and without much to say.

Poetisin'

Michael Richardson

In a moment, I
    Or in a decade
will pitch forward into the earth
of my garden
the ground will rise to meet me shut-eyed

I will step onto a night train
eastbound
my cold feet in cold air
sticking my hand out the gap and then
feeling fingers numb like packed snow
standing close to the boiler watching dark fields of the desert roll
by

and soon desert sprouts a city
whose name I can't pronounce
    yet
ayn-dab-dab-a
shoorlty
shooyani

the signs are written

    in no language I know

I step into a car with people from the train
They are

    loud and elegant
And smell of salt
We are friends, but I do not know them

    yet

we dance in low rooms and I watch them drink from
smoking bowls
later we walk down stairs carved into the mountainside
headed home and drunk
a young man talks to a demon

    behind a stone door
in the morning I walk by a fleet of coracles, bobbing in
the tide

    they are meant for children

I watch a man spread a napkin

    in a cafe
make an incision

    by knife and fork

Poetisin' | *Michael Richardson*

and bite into a bicycle
    with relish

the soft rains come and go
falling in the desert
I remember how to pronounce the city
    And

In a moment, he
    Or in a decade
who made the land sing
    will ask me if I want
and I will tell him no.

Discipline

Xiaoran Shi

One, two, three, four, five.
One, two, three, four, five, six, sev—
Oh, fuck. Three, four, five.

Backgarden, Three O'clock

Finn Gabriel Keogh

Though the sun is slanted now,
at three o'clock, there still lies a
spot midway down the garden,
where specks (winged insects)
swirl in bouts,
and are similar to thin flashes
of hair-like webs draping
tenuously over grass.
Here, there is a clear mark
between
the realm of fence-shadow and
the agapanthus,
side-lit by the low arcing sun:
dark green lines are drawn
across each blade-leaf
and there are two images of the
same green—
one blue with the cool of shade and reflected sky,

cloudless and perfectly coloured,
one lit full through by white-gold.

I know I cannot see it,
but I still feel that the air amid this scene
is humming with the same force
that makes such full hues in the agapanthus.

And if I let my lids droop,
and upturn my face,
I am kissed on both and my forehead
as no one can kiss me.

Now, a dozen moments later,
small clouds in the west, white-rimmed,
and the sense of the sky and late afternoon world,
lined and fringed with light,
being pressed softly up against me,
and shimmering thinly just below the water of my mind.

Later still, a low rosy sky,
rose clouds, and southerly
a short arc of wings.

Manfred Variations

Jonathan Dunk

I

The mountain shudders beneath
Emptiness untouched,
But for cloud-stroke,
And sleepless thought.

In wisps of narcotic twilight,
Iblis sings a pale song,
The echo
Whispers your name.

The cruel music remembers
your touch,
A tap on the chair in your study,
A scent of tea and honey,
The sweet unsilence of breath.

Light is my brother.
Your room is barred.

Frost blooms in the hearth.
Where I burnt the piano.
I live and live alone.

II
And I heard a song in the light of a newborn star
And followed through velvet flung night.
At the tip of a galaxy's whorl
I found her.
Daughter of light, daughter of air
Chill-glass tongue, comet-wake hair

Infinity, sweet madness,
Clasped in her eye,
Her song was thought-music
Unselved.
Listening I wept, listening I fell
Through the shadow of heaven, and the limit of hell.

Through time-worlds unknit I sank
To the womb of music
Unheard.
In symphony of light before light
I fell through death into flight.

And I touched the face of a dying God

Down on Halifax

Nicholas Fahy

A man whose English was severely broken, much like the rest of his figure, had taken me through Bosnia and Slovakia, but an unfortunate incident involving a Rolls Royce and a few poorly chosen words strewn together in some remote Slavic dialect relieved me of my guide's services and left me to wander northwest until I reached Belarus. Here, there was nothing but short days and an endless torrential rain. Money had become problematic; my line of credit had been rejected. I began to feel as if some unknown force were leading me across Europe, taunting and provoking me, a mere marionette caught within a city of darkness. Alighting from a Broadfast locomotive in Vitebsk and feeling thus, I sought refuge within a hostel in the British quarter, down on Halifax Avenue.

'Čamu dzvie ruki! Čamu dzvie ruki!' He slammed his fist into the wall and a faint tremble shook the furniture. Long locks of black hair, finely coated in sweat, hung over his bowed head. Silence surrounded. He was leaning against the wall, breathing deeply. Then, 'Čamu dzvie ruki!' again in heavy White Ruthenian and another fist slammed against the wall, the man's entire body wrenching with the exertion. Blood dripped from his hands.

'He keeps asking, "Why two hands?"', explained Mr Pratt, my fellow lodger, pausing between languid puffs of his pipe. He was reclined in a corner of the room on a mattress, watching with dull curiosity the tortured figure before him. 'No need to panic I should think.'

'Oughtn't we do something?' I enquired, eyes wide and perspiring through my jacket.

'No, no. We all have such demons.' Mr Pratt was now absentmindedly playing with a ring on his finger. 'Best to leave Rafters here to his own design. No good could possibly come of any intervention.' To me it looked as if there were a butterfly moulded on the ring, only its wings were warped horrifically, a tragically melted beauty. I deduced the ring was a remnant from some lost love of Mr Pratt's, who was quite possibly dead, or quite possibly unable to handle the listless gaze of a man jaded in accomplishment, now intolerable to the commonalities of everyday life—either way, the ring had been hostage to an ensuing fire.

'Čamu dzvie ruki!' and the man threw himself against the wall, this time a smear of blood marking the contact of delicate flesh against hard drywall, his will and exertion culminating in a scream of terrible, terrible anguish.

I was leaning against the bookshelf with a quickened breath, my palms damp against the cool wood. Until this moment I had never seen the man's eyes, for he lodged across the hall, a quiet man who kept to himself. Back from an unsuccessful meeting with a Royal Dutch Bank manager, I had been greeted by the sight of this dark, unshaven man, sweat-covered and with clothes torn, berating himself against the wall of my room, Mr Pratt looking on with an occasional smile. But now the man, Rafters as Mr Pratt informed me the lodgers called him, turned to confront me, the entire immensity of his body still throbbing with his exertions. And how does one describe what words have never described before? For the man's eyes were of a colour only likened to violets set beneath the rays of a cold sunset. They were eyes of a colour, yes, but hardly, for they lacked all sense of clarity.

I averted my gaze from the man, lest he should see me as a combatant to his ravings, yet I could feel him looking at me. Mr Pratt was now tossing a coin up and down in the air, catching it in the palm of his hand. He seemed not to have noticed our entanglement. My breath caught, my pulse deadened. Silence again surrounded.

'Čamu abiedzvie ruki na hadzinnik?' Rafters was now speaking in a calm voice, rational and methodical, but noticeably restrained. I looked blankly back at him and shook my head. I had no knowledge of Belarusian. He seemed to think I was responding to the question. His eyes flickered slightly, a twitch, as if his restraint were breaking down. He took a step closer. For me there would be no retreat, I was backed against the bookshelf. I tried in vain to gesture my incomprehension.

'Čamu abiedzvie ruki na hadzinnik?' This time there was a tremble in his voice. Not a submission, but a wall as it collapses from anarchy.

'I'm sorry, but I do not understand you. I cannot help.'

His hand made a movement towards me, but he caught himself with the other hand and made as if he were adjusting a tear in his shirt. As he did so I saw the ink stains on the palms of his hands.

Mr Pratt did not even look up from his coin tossing. 'He asks you: "Why two hands on a clock?"'

'Why two hands on a clock?'

The man looked at me, knowing that I understood him at last. He looked expectant, but an expectancy denoting that he would afford me a crazed and irrational response, regardless of the answer I provided. The locks of his hair gleamed across his face, he straightened his back and his breath steadied.

'I'm not quite sure. I don't know really. But I suppose there must be several answers.' I made an emphatic gesture to the man, evidencing my uncertainty.

At this he let out a truly terrible cry and turned to the wall once more to throw his fist deep into the gold trim, so much so that the wall audibly cracked and relented. His eyes were deeply infused with anger as, turning, he once more took me in. His breathing was now rushed, rampant, on the edge of the edge of the edge and then he came for me, running and throwing his body at full force. For what's it worth, my agility did not fail me, and although this man's crazed behaviour, I concede, did both shock and scare me, I managed to evade his attack and sought refuge upon the mattress with Mr Pratt. The man had looked up from his coin-toss just in time to witness my disposition, but still bore an expression of languid boredom.

'Still no need to panic?' I threw at him, angered at the calmness of his manner.

Rafters was getting up slowly, having gone right through one of the shelves which, splintering and cracking at odd angles, caused a deep red depression to be borne on his forehead. His temperament had become much calmer after this shock. His feet stumbled as my writing desk became the object of his support.

Mr Pratt began flicking through a worn paperback.

As my breath steadied once more, anger subsiding, I looked across the room at Rafters. He was staring back at me, that deep intensity not lost from his gaze. I felt suddenly very alone. With both palms on the writing desk, he spoke to me once more.

'Čamu my navat nazyvajem ich rukach?'

' "Why do we even call them hands?" ' translated Mr Pratt. He had noticed a beetle caught between the paperback's pages.

'Why do we call them hands?' I considered. 'Well, I suppose it's because they are referential objects. A clock's hands point to numbers just as we gesture with our hands. There is a certain similarity between the actions of a clock and the goings on of people. The meaning is probably as simple as that.'

Rafters seemed to take this answer as once again insufficient, for he looked at me more seriously with each syllable that Mr Pratt translated. Upon the conclusion he came towards me. Slowly, deliberately, measuredly. His restraint was clearly on the verge of breaking from its tether. He proceeded to place an arm on my shoulder and whispered directly into my face, the alcohol on his breath revolting my senses.

'I can't understand him either,' was all Mr Pratt could say to my look of expectancy.

I thought that at any instant I would feel the great terror of this brute's bloodied fist slamming into my face and knocking me out cold, and then what? Killing me right there on the floor? In front of the sorely-in-need-of-light-hearted-entertainment Mr Pratt? Would he just sit there and flicker his smile occasionally? I saw my body outstretched on the floor, horribly contorted, the blood having congealed where my nose had been broken, blood seeping out of the sockets of my eyes, bruises across my chest, teeth marks on my neck and running the length of my arms...

But no, Rafters merely formed a polite smile, patted me on the shoulder and returned to the writing desk, proceeding to beat his head against the wall, running his bloodied fist up and down the length of the wallpaper and loudly questioning the absurdity of the temporal recording process.

Thoughts were too many at this stage and I really was unsure as to what to do with myself, the probability that I would survive the night, the irrationality of the man beating his head on the hardboard in front of me and the small beetle being twirled between Mr Pratt's fingers, all great concerns which troubled me.

'I must return some stationery to Mr Endell's room,' I quickly resolved, informing Mr Pratt as I alighted from the mattress, seized the borrowed ink jar and paper from atop my suitcase and briskly left the room.

Outside in the corridor I could still hear the dull thud of Rafters as he continued his vigil, his deep moan piercing my skin and sending a sharp chill to the base of my spine. I walked along the red velvet, damp with the comings and goings of the hostel patrons, and proceeded towards the staircase that led to the landlord's upstairs quarters. Halfway up the staircase I heard the voice of Mr Pratt calling to me, so I descended once again, receiving him through the grills of the handrail.

'You know that it is all to do with subject matter, right?' His voice was measured, strangely devoid of resonance in the small hallway.

'I'm sorry?'

'Rafters. His pleas for answers. It's all to do with subject matter.'

'How so?'

'Well, how could it not be?'

'But what should it matter why clocks have two hands? Why should he think it matters? What's wrong with him?'

'Well I charge you, why should it not mean the world to that man? Really, I'm sure you know as well as I do, that there are some things that should never be said, some questions that should never be asked.' He paused and from afar I could see him start at the gaze of the portrait beside him, his body briefly aquiver before returning to its natural languidness. 'Prospects really seem limited from the inside, don't they?'

The tolling of the Grand Winchester filled the cavity of the narrow hallway. I shouted my reply, but Mr Pratt had already gone. So, left alone in the hallway with my own subject matter very much pressing deeply against the walls of my mind, I shook my head and ascended towards Mr Endell's room.

Outside his quarters, stationery implements in hand, I knocked several times but gained no reply. No light escaped beneath the door, so I turned as if to depart, assuming the man to be absent, when I heard a low rumble from the interior of the apartment. It seemed the sound of a hammer rising and falling, rising and falling, audibly intensifying. But the sound of the surface the hammer was striking was indiscernible, a screeching sound, like that of nails to a blackboard, like a sound that died very slowly. And then came the sound of groaning. A woman. Deep sensual groans of pleasure which resonated throughout the entire room, escaping beneath the thin gap between door and floor, and flooding the hallway, enveloping me from all sides, binding me.

After several minutes of eavesdropping on such turbulent sounds, my curiosity indelibly aroused, the woman's pleasurable groaning began to assume a decidedly more sinister tone, morphing into that of a horrid scream.

And then the hammer fell. And then the hammer rose. And then it fell once more. And I knew that I had to promptly leave this raw scream, this contented evocation of death, hurriedly discarding the borrowed stationery on a nearby table.

Down on Halifax | *Nicholas Fahy*

I descended the stairs, thoroughly unnerved and with sweat having once more accrued on my forehead. My jacket caught on the handrail and tore slightly in my haste. When I reached the bottom of the staircase my feet sank beneath what had become two inches of water, chilling my ankles. It filled the hallway in both directions.

Why two hands?

I laid blame on the torrential rain. In addition, one of the lights had burned out in my absence, filling the far end of the hallway with an enveloping darkness. With this, I craved the refuge of my apartment.

As I neared my door a candelabra lay askew on the red velvet, its candlesticks scattered and slowly floating down the corridor. The neck of the candelabra was bent awkwardly, kinked, as if it had fallen with great force from the three foot table adjacent and then beaten, roughly, back into shape. It was too heavy to be taken by the current and it merely lay deadened, half submerged beneath the water. Tiny gold flakes of its skin rested on the water's surface, lolling after the candlesticks in shimmery pursuit, like mourners after a hearse.

Why two hands?

I picked up the maimed candelabra and replaced it on the table, its half-eroded facade deplorable in the half-light. The brass doorknob to my room beckoned, and as I inserted the key and turned I felt the lock slip out of place. I kept turning and with each revolution the knob verged on opening and then fell once more into irretrievable circularity. Rising water now completely filled my shoes as the turning never ceased, on and on and on and click and click and click and nothing, nothing but regularity, the regular ticking over of a broken lock, backgrounded by the soft trickle of a stream.

And then I fell through the door, the brass handle having disintegrated in my hand, and I was back in my apartment. I sighed with relief and settled for propping the door closed with a chair. It almost felt like home, a sanctuary, somewhere warm and inviting after the cold of a day. There was still water here, but not quite as bad as in the hallway, an inch at most. And it was lukewarm as it seeped through the gaps between the leather of my shoes. Rain was coming in through the window, filling up the small guttering beneath the sill and running down the wall and into the small ocean that became my room. I moved to shut it. The noise outside was tremendous, the wind a howling pack of wolves, and its friend, the darkness, formidable and intimidating.

Why two hands?

As soon as the pane closed the room fell utterly silent. I could still see the rain rapping against the sill, the gutter now overflowing onto the pavement and, visually, nature made a tumultuous noise. But inside I could hear nothing.

I relaxed and took off my coat, thought better of lighting the fireplace and lay down on my mattress, spread-eagled across the sheets. Mr Pratt's mattress lay as dishevelled as before, the paperback atop the blankets and, in pyramid form, the dead beetle on top.

It was then that I noticed the stains. There was a line of blood running down the side of the bookshelf, a dark red, richer than the velvet of the carpeted hallways. It swelled and rushed towards the ocean of water that was the floor and upon meeting it, dispersed into thousands of tiny red spirals, bubbles forming. I followed the path of the blood, which ran not towards the door and the escape it offered, but towards the writing desk, clumping in large pools around the desk legs, grossly discolouring the wood. I surmised that Rafters' earlier ranting must have damaged the wall.

I approached the desk, my feet wet and covered in blood, and crouched down to peer beneath the table in the hope of finding the hole the bloodied water so desperately sought. Foamy red bubbles were forming against the back of the wall, but in the dim light it was too difficult to discern any impairment. Momentarily I lost my balance as I rose and my hand grazed the bloodied water. I gripped onto the desk to prevent myself from falling into the foamy mess and while doing so, realised, with great perplexity, that the lock to the drawer was open.

Once upright I opened the drawer. It slid out with a dull creak to reveal two hands, sawn off at the wrists, their bloody stumps still freshly leaking throughout, bones protruding alongside severed nerves. I screamed out in panic, mortified. The blood was yet to congeal, indicating they had been only recently sawn off, but the putrid smell already engulfed me. The fingers were straight, displayed elegantly in their pool of blood, pointing to the rear of the drawer. Trembling and shaking, I reached in and groped a small placard, soaking in blood. Upon it, in frightened handwriting, was the once elegant script of an English gentleman, reading: 'Why two hands?'.

And, again surveying the horrid contents of the drawer, I espied the silver glisten of a once beautiful ring, now horrifically contorted beyond redemption, most likely having burned in solitude at the bottom of a grate, and, most notably, bearing a pair of warped butterfly wings.

I Looked on My Right Hand, and Beheld

Rafi Alam

Nothing moved in this room,
bar the flowers that discreetly
shook when spent feet
silently thudded outside;

Die! not here: a room with grey-blue
walls and speckled vinyl floors
that squeaked under plastic feet,
a room redolent of lavender and
urine;

Barren hours float past
day after day after month,
people walk in and out of this room,
carrying clipboards and trays;

Rays crept in past pitted curtains,
and I wrote in this light

I Looked on My Right Hand, and Beheld | *Rafi Alam*

a word per day—it was secret
from nurses and the few guests;

'Blessed is the tortoise.'
Betwixt each word I recalled:
every moment recalled a hundred memories,
every day was a hundred lifetimes;

Night-time awoke to a trance until daytime,
fashioning dreams upon sight,
and out of these visions I constructed
the word I would write for the day;

Braving my memories I traced
sunbathed thighs on a patio
and laughter, drinking—it was summer.
In winter, I was alone;

'Atone.' The phone would ring
as the vision changed, and her voice
would escort me through the
Dreams. I was never alone here;

Here in this room with grey-blue
walls and speckled vinyl floors

that squeaked under plastic feet,
a room redolent of lavender and urine;

Foreign in my carcass,
I forget the disease that crippled me
to this, but how can I forget the
lost devotion that makes me?

'Ye shall know the truth ...' she said.
Beyond the tears that knocked
against eyelids like shut doors,
awoke a sorrow from its dormancy;

Urgently I asked questions—
she shook her head, 'you'll understand
one day on the borderlines of blindness
... and the truth shall set you free'.

Weak and trapped amongst sterile bedsheets
chaining me to ill health, I was told there's
no way out, and I lay in bed in stasis
wondering what she meant for this;

Piss and flowers, walls,
between words each weighing eternity,

I Looked on My Right Hand, and Beheld | *Rafi Alam*

I tore at the strata of heartache,
until I found the bowels of sickness;

Christmas, Easter, birthdays:
Time passes by slowly, but
Death too quickly—the heavy
Hand of Doom hovers closely;

Mostly I lie down amongst recollections of every
word she said … This rotten bed entombs all pathetic
memories of the past—as
Poetry is the art of suffering as cartography:
only the sick can write,
only the healthy read.

When You Come 'Round

Danielle Chiaverini

Wanderer; breach arc and scale
—half a hemisphere, come
autumn
time to settle in.
Grubby blonde rain colliding
with
last season's speckled hen,
you know what I mean.
Let in former ache; waning
petulance
beset by all emotion?
Floodgates
of feeling clang/Szechuan
steaming by
—no, no, no, no, no,
reach opulent heights then calm
(or forced to be by rampant greenery).
Pages turn; hearts hang on fishing wire
and twirl. Every movement now feels comfortable.

When You Come 'Round | *Danielle Chiaverini*

Haystacks like hard lights, do not panic
your white whimper. Begin to shake!
Belly-pit buzzing, christen
this day with bold eyes
before the mirror.
Nature is disguise for passion
of the brain, man-made
(automotives and such).
A vestibule. Let the story drop.

The Werther Effect

James Watson

I

It was morning and a pig had trapped itself in the well. Everest had never seen a pig before: he was a city boy, from London. And now, after the death of his wife, he had come to Nigeria as a missionary.

They could not see the pig because it was not yet noon and the shadows were covering the hole; yet they could hear the oinks and squeals of the beast in the pit. Even if Everest had seen a pig in London it would be a much different creature to the one in the well. In London, pigs are herded, bred, and cultured; here, they were wild beasts. Seeing a pig in Kenya would be like seeing a grizzly bear in the Rocky Mountains (which he had once seen, with his wife, on a trip to America). It sounded as if it was hurt, as if it had broken something during the fall down. Maybe it had broken its neck. Can pigs break their necks? He had never heard of one doing such, but he had also never seen a pig.

The natives wanted to kill it, but could not kill it in their well. They were gathering ropes and they were going to lower a man into the well in order to tie up the pig and lift it out of the well. At least this was what Everest thought: he had not yet learned the language. In fact, it was the natives who adapted to him—in the three months he had been there most of the natives (at least the elders of the tribe) had formed a basic understanding of English. It wasn't the same English he spoke at home—surprisingly the natives had adopted American accents and pronunciations—but an avenue of communication had been opened. But now they spoke in their native tongue and he stood there now like an awkward clown who wasn't in on the inside joke.

'What are you doing?' asked Everest.

One of the elders looked back at him: 'Broken pig at bottom of the well. Can't get blood into water.'

Everest didn't know his name. He didn't know any of their names. He had been told them on his first day at the camp, but there were so many apostrophes, double a's, and clickings of the tongue that he forfeited any real attempt to understand what they were saying and arranged them by physical attributes: short, skinny, tall, shaved head, nose ring.

And now Tall Earring was lowering Skinny Cheek-Scar into the well. It wasn't too far down, maybe ten feet. There had been water in the well in winter, but it hadn't rained since his arrival and there must have been no more than six inches. This equated to roughly two and a half litres of water (or one week before they would have to find a new source)

Skinny Cheek-Scar was yelling something up to Tall Earring. 'What's he saying?'

'Pig neck broken.'

Skinny Cheek-Scar yelled three short yelps and the natives began to tug on the rope. Everest was old now, seventy-one years old. His gut was bloated, his thinning hair was grey-white, and his fingers were short stubby cigars. If he had tried to lift up the pig he would have broken his back. So he watched as the entire tribe tugged at the cord of rope. The strongest of them leaned back as if they were rowers, while the weaker simply held onto the fibres like a child holds onto his father's hand.

Skinny Cheek-Scar came out first. His face was covered with blood and the natives retreated a step back in shock and let their grip loosen. This gave momentum back to the weight of the pig and nearly dragged Skinny Cheek-Scar back into the well but he kept his balance. He turned around and pulled on the rope. The rest of the tribe had stopped: they were still terrified by the sight of him. Not only was his face covered with blood, but he had cuts and scratches down the course of his back. Skinny Cheek-Scar was now the rower, using his weight to lift up this near-dead or already-dead beast. He feet scuttled, trying to get the best stance. He was leaning much further back than any other member of his tribe, his body leaning parallel to the earth. His shadow crawled along the dirt and moved with him as he lifted the pig out of the well.

The body flopped onto the dirt ground. It had two broken legs and a broken neck, and most of its skin had been ripped from its face and torso. It had left a trail of blood from the well and what was left of the water was now gone. But it was still alive: its ears flicked, its tongue slithered, and the pupils gave away small measurements of movement. In its eyes ... there was something about its eyes. Out here in the Kenyan heat, where the sun was nearing its zenith, the light seemed to enter its eyes at a peculiar angle. Deep inside it must be reflecting or refracting—ricocheting around the iris, the pupil, the corneas. They were illuminated, as if being caught in the headlights. Everest watched them as the elder prepared to kill the pig.

II

They had just had dinner and it was now time for their meeting in the tent. Every day, after they had their nightly meal which usually consisted of beans and wild meat (but tonight many stuck with just the vegetarian option as the scene of the pig earlier had left a dead taste swishing around their taste buds), Everest was supposed to give the people a speech based on a story from the Bible. Everest, awkwardly, was an atheist, so his speeches usually were made up of events from his life or funny films he had seen back in London. He told them stories of England winning the World Cup, or relayed to them the entire Star Wars saga (both prequels and sequels).

This was how the night started. He was close to the end of Episode V and his crowd seemed to be enamoured with him. They loved his stories: tales of good versus evil, of the little guy coming out on top, of the luck of finding a twenty-pound note right there in the middle of the street. Despite his success as a raconteur, he had never once been able to make his audience laugh. While tales of drama typically translated well from culture to tribe to race, humour was an indecipherable beast—one which seemed to originate not from the stomach but down past the knees, the place down there which kept one's core beliefs and values, the cave which hid your forgotten treasures: the reasons you went to school, or church, or the motives for your signs of affection. The things he could not put into words. It was not a case of lost in translation (to use a cliché) but rather the natives never laughed at his jokes because they did not consider Everest's most dear items with the same affection that he did. And so, after many failed attempts to rise a chuckle or a smirk from the deep throats of these cloth-wearing, tattoo-scarred natives, he stopped trying. And within this world without comedy and laughter, his mind took a turn to much darker things.

'Many of you know that I was married back in England to a woman, but she died before I came here.' Staring out into the small, oval faces of the crowd, he felt as if tears were building up in the back of his eye sockets. 'Yes, married for twenty years. I told you she died of illness but that's not true. She killed herself, shot herself with a gun. She decided she didn't want to live anymore.' He felt as if he was going to collapse into a mess of self-pity. Tears were stockpiling themselves within him. And that's when it happened, the sight which he had longed to see ever since he got here, the feature of this desert world which he had been forced to do without. It began with a young man in the front who spread his lips and filled his mouth with teeth. Like a contagion, it spread from man to woman to child, all of them widening their chafed and peeling lips, opening their mouths, and exposing their teeth. From the back began a wild holler which erupted volcanically, echoing and reverberating within the confines of the tent. It spread among the locals and Everest realised what was happening: there were laughing, laughing at him.

'Wh—What are you doing? Why are you laughing?'

Skinny Cheek-Scar approached and in between cascades of laughter, managed to form the words: 'You people kill yourselves.

Why do you do it? We kill hyenas, we kill boars, we kill lions, but we do not kill ourselves. That's stupid.'

The laughter swallowed up the natives like a whirlpool, with men and women literally rolling on the dirt floor. Some even held their sides as if they would burst.

'But... But why is this funny?'

They wouldn't answer. They couldn't. Everest left the tent and walked outside like a barbarian at a modern art gallery. He had never been so furious in his life. He was at the centre of the camp and began to walk south. The last beams of the sun were hitting the horizon and the borders of the camp, a near-perfect circle marked out with small, iridescent stones glowing like the pig's eyes and Everest thought to himself, *Why am I here? What did I expect to occur?* And he looked behind him and saw his shadow slowly evaporating into the darkness and thought, *I have been out here all my life.*

Sketch of Saxophone Solo

Joel Mak

This Montréalais saxophonist is
everywhere
he is Everyone
he is John Coltrane of 21st
century
he is
everywhere—man
and he's hitting notes that he
shouldn't hit

notes
of paloozas and katankerous kaklings
of high hats
and deep sea vibrations of the double bass—frantic
running
of piano lines
black white black black black white white black white
white wh wh wh white
blang kerblang bling!

high screeech note!
deep breath—
five runs zig zags in the air of a speakeasy
six voluminous blasts of the horn
shockwaves in a San Franciscan street all the way from
Canada
seven disjointed claps from four
high
men
cigarettes hanging from their lips
never been inhaled
some sorta fog in the air
thick at head level
but dispersing as it rises
Col-trane
butterflies
blips in the air by butterflies
fa-flapfliterryflap
and he starts his run again
his eyes have been shut for the past two minutes
—a child's reaction to lightning and Thor's drumming
and he's off—to unchartered territories

hushing heated arguments in cold Montréal street
in fast forward motion

Sketch of Saxophone Solo | *Joel Mak*

finalising the wills of dying Stephen Dedaluses
pharyngeal wails—free jazz is free will

wobbles & wallops the buzzed up compact jazz bar air
finishing his solo with a few wandering wading drowning
crotchets (Red Riding Hood
bopping popping bubble gum
the Wolf whimpers
& the house of cards
they fall down)

cause he's gliding back to earth
Montréal's Coltrane—[Koltrã]

a huge gust of wind
a naked tree far off bristles
it'll start snowing soon—the first flakes of winter
the train slows down—pulls into its last stop at Honoré
Beaugrand
people hurry home necks shrunk fists clenched in
pockets

Col—
trane
phhhrroooang hush

hoots & phreeeeewits! & thunderous applause
from the drunk & sober &
from the tone deaf

—& even Jesus reached for His inhaler
on rue St. Denis.

A Hard Day's Knight

Dashiell Moore

Sydney University. A symbol of colonial pride, the sandstone grandeur of the university lecture halls was awe-inspiring. They made him feel part of something important; his studies were worthwhile. Like a drowning man desperately clawing his way to the surface for air, Otieno threw himself into ANHS1602: Greek and Roman Mythology. Away from his studies however, under the jacaranda in the Quad, Otieno found the rest of campus life discomforting. Making friends, meeting girls, negotiating the gentrified inner city was difficult. Reality felt superficial in comparison to the literary depths through which he ventured, full of wonder, full of dreams, holes in those pockets, and hats leaking darkness. The present held only compromises for Otieno.

Our hero lived in the filthy squalor of shabby, shared households, waking beneath scratchy sheets to the smell of re-heated coffee. Otieno's alarm was the sound of the Western XPT rattling his window, a signal for the rising day. He dressed himself from his closet away from home—the couch, scrunched his work into his bag and headed out, usually foregoing proper breakfasts and goodbyes.

Otieno met Eros in Fisher Library. Their meeting was odd. Otieno had never felt deep platonic love so it surprised him that it would first meet him in the gathering dust of archives and manuscripts in the library stacks. He knew he was going the wrong way about things, finding love through Ancient Romance, through Shakespeare and Homer, a fraud. He was looking for historical and literary coherence in his end-of-semester essay rather than gripping the rose between his teeth.

Eros was Otieno's favorite god—it was just something about his sub-Olympian position, his always unreliable favours and tireless, if fickle labour. Feeding his infatuation, Otieno rode on a wave of mythology. On Tuesdays and Thursdays he caught the train home, fuzzy with cheap beer and hot chips. His head caught in the swaying tides of alcohol, clear sight evaded him. He saw his reflection on yellowing panes of glass, a brown-haired bookworm; used to wear glasses. Where would Eros be, at this moment? What would he be doing? He murmured to himself, 'Eros's eyelids faltered under the measurement of night.' Otieno grew drowsy and bumped his head, asleep against the pane. Mentally, he wrote:

Eros' eyelids faltered under the measurement of night; there was no tangible end. He craved stillness, and yet his task was all around him, amplifying the sound of footsteps, back heel, front toe. He could not falter, could not stop for a moment, or he'd fall—and the world with him. But tonight, his menial love-tasks had so far consisted of stale popcorn, dark cinemas, Toyotas in backalleys.

The next morning Otieno woke in a crusty slump on the couch, with a biting hangover and smelling of ink and beer. He rose from the creaking springs of the couch, uncomfortably sticky. He desperately needed a shower and shave. 'Do you think using Ancient History as personal therapy is sad?' The bathroom mirror (his usual confidante) didn't reply, and Otieno cut himself with his razor. He swore, and with no toilet paper to stop the flow of blood on his chin, walked out into the world.

Without really thinking, Otieno was merging with the primordial god of sexual love. Eros was more fun to talk with than stern Tacitus. Otieno's own formless nature lent him to mirror his influences, his books, and his landscape. The gods invigorated Otieno, who poured his heart into what he felt was a brilliant end-of-semester Ancient History essay. He was deflated when he received a shameful borderline fail: 'This is an overly personal account—the question asked for a critical appraisal of the literary text, not a pseudo-Greek Mythology of your own imagination ... Please rewrite.'

He had written:

A Hard Day's Knight by Otieno Hamilton (SID 37690766)

Through the night, Eros accomplished his Herculean tasks, one by one. Arms hung in pairs; lips brushed and reached over one another, lips searching for what lay beyond. Bodies filling each other's dips and bumps, forming intricate puzzles for Eros to solve.

JACK: I love you baby.

JILL: Love me tender. [Giggles]

Forget about the pair of them, do it and be done, Eros thought. Her name might be Jill, or Linda, or Sue; she could wait. He would undoubtedly see her again, presumably with another man. Eros was tired of the sight of banal adulteries, leaving after breathing love in and out. Starlight twinkled across his back, and the tremor of human heartbeats fluttered inside his brain. Tired now, Eros spun around the cosmos, towards the dawning summer sky. He looked down on rooftops and heard the girl cry.

The Fates cackled at Otieno's academic failure, his possibilities and his life, weaving him into a gaudy tapestry, his future. It had happened like this: leaving the stuffy lecture theatre, someone bumped into him from behind. Otieno lurched into a wheelie-bin, dropped his textbooks and rolled his ankle. A press of students behind him. Swore. He felt a hand on his shoulder. The image in the mirror now slowed. She had bent down to Otieno's level. 'Um, you dropped your books. (Pause) Here—are you okay?' Her lips had quirked to one side there (Otieno replayed her quizzical gesture a few times in the mirror, his body still). She handed his books back to him. He murmured 'thanks'.

'I'm Fiona,' she said.

Otieno furrowed his brow, exchanging a silent blessing and hello, like change in a pocket.

'I'm Otieno.'

But his words were swallowed up in the throng of chattering, leather-clad creative Arts students streaming past him from ancient Seneca to sunlight and cheap coffee. Otieno stood smitten. He thought of Eros' own desires—forever working, bestowing favors, and by definition never satisfied. He could relate to that.

Eros expressed earthly passion in all its dimensions, but was himself constantly pierced by both desire and a biting jealousy. He would give his blessed breath upon earth for a moment of fleshly desires, to be so easily satisfied.

Night. Otieno yawned and dropped the page in his lap, spilling the light in shadows around him, like the ceiling fan of his childhood bedroom. He levered himself and his pile of notes up from the couch, accidentally knocking over the one good floor-lamp in the grungy, communal loungeroom. Swearing, he dumped his stuff on the carpet, went to take a piss, opened the fridge and drank some milk from the carton. Thankfully it wasn't the expired milk that still lay pungent on the table. Returning to the lounge, he settled down again and reached for pen and paper. He needed to write, to think. He couldn't sleep. There was always someone awake around him, laughter from the jumping bedroom down the corridor. Something was bugging him. Otieno flattened his ears, and then twisted the fallen lampshade over his head, asleep over the poem he had written a moment before.

The girl pauses at the bus stop.

She unravels herself.

Her modesty,

Wrapping it around her femininity.

A Fragile Object stepped onto the bus, exposed to

A Hard Day's Knight | *Dashiell Moore*

EXPLICIT! ILLICIT! DROOLING HOBBESIAN BOYS...

The drool gathered up in the winds of air conditioning,

Hit her in the forehead.

Down it fell, into her frown

Red-faced

Love began.

Otieno woke, hot and light-headed. He sensed that, despite Eros' expressions, his god would always feel frustration or longing, for earthly women couldn't see him, and so would be insensible to his charms. That was it! He too would have to accept this, learn restraint, patience, wisdom. Otieno felt lighter, almost freer in the thought. He gripped his pen, rubbing writing calluses into fingertips, knocking over empty cereal boxes in the process, and resting his elbow into the sour milk stain. The loungeroom by daybreak was a sty of half-filled exercise books and melted chocolate ice-cream. He was accustomed to wading through mess to write; but today, he exercised a new-felt clarity. He picked up his literary flotsam from the floor and dumped it in a neat pile next to the couch. His house was only a short train-ride to uni, and for once he wasn't late for lectures. Stretching to the pavement and the light, he walked briskly to the station, breathing in misty fire.

The next four days were spent in silent reconnaissance. Otieno slowly formed an image of his love. She flooded him with sensation. He felt his internal chemistry changing.

The girl Fiona was smooth porcelain giving way to tanned pine, dainty fingers garnished with six rings and a star; her eyes twinkled with gold dust circling green. Her feet were encircled with a beaded anklet, green-glitter toe-nail polish, matching designer thongs. It seemed everything about her was in companionship with something else.

They say that, long ago, Eros battled with Thanatos, that hateful shepherd of the dead. Between their conflicts lay the delicate balance of the human condition. As they fought, the hearts of the citizens clenched, arteries bleached grey. Their life force draining, people slumped where they stood. Sleeping infants woke up whimpering, with no one in sight. Something was out of place, out of kilter.

Against Thanatos' compelling downwards pull, Eros edged back, gaining some momentum. He began to stretch out limbs, like swimming under water, grasping all proportions of space available to reach.

Otieno's notebooks were now stretched and taut, thrown like mooring lines around an old bollard. It was Sunday night, two days of missed classes last week had collated with the dense vegetation of the lounge, its putrid smell seeping out the window. Over the weekend, a furious introspection had penetrated his psyche: only the disgusting room remained a constant. But his Ancient History essay was finally done, and by the due date. And it was impressive. He'd nailed Eros. Those history books just didn't appreciate Eros' labours—his epic battle with Thanatos, the need for psychic balance in the world. He smiled to himself as he slurped extra Lynx roll-on under his arms. Most importantly, Otieno felt firm, supple, 'Not bad,' he said to himself in the bathroom mirror, twinkling the edges of his mouth, turning out his creases. He caught himself looking for too long, and chuckled to himself, 'You're all ego!'

Monday afternoon, Archaeology Method II. Otieno itched in his seat, deliriously preoccupied. Right now he knew Fiona was just a hundred metres away in her own tutorial. He was invigorated, laughingly copying down the words 'hello' and 'goodbye' from his tutor in his notepad. The tutorial finally over, he swept out of the room and down the old steps. He cut across the freshly cut quadrangle lawn, passing students resting and murmuring through sleepy mouths the disappearing mornings of their life. He knew that Fiona would be coming out of her Art History tute. Would she

be heading to the bar? Yes, there she was. He could feel his heart
beating, reverberating on the roof of his mouth as they drew close.

'Fiona!' He caught her eye and held it. She was perfect. 'Hi,
uh—how are you? Feel like some food?'

'Sure, I'm starving. Manning?'

Otieno nodded and they moved off together.

The Manning balcony was only half full. Otieno bought chips
and coffee, and they gravitated to a quiet corner. Sat, munched,
sipped, chatted. Fiona was talking about her Art History essay,
also due today, and, yes, she'd finished it. Select and evaluate
an important sculpture in the context of twentieth-century
iconography.

'What did you choose?'

'I couldn't decide—then I remembered my year eleven trip
to Europe, and how I loved travelling the London Underground.
It's totally brilliant. And I just chose this random statue that I
remember was above the station near our hotel. Have you seen it?
I've got a picture on my phone. It's kind of nice, don't you think?'

Otieno looked at the winged figure of the golden archer above
Piccadilly Circus. Nude, swift and victorious, glowing in the sun.
His heart soared.

'Anteros,' Fiona smiled.

'But that's—Eros!' Otieno gasped.

'Everyone says that. No, it's his brother. Heaps of people make
that mistake.'

Otieno felt his ground slipping, embarrassed. Archaeology and
myth surrendering to modernity.

'He's much nicer than Eros; not so lonely and complicated. He's
the god of requited love, you see. And you know what? He also
punishes those who scorn love—it's true! I Wiki'd it yesterday.'

'Yeah, he looks kind of cool.'

*Eros would give his blessed breath upon Earth for a moment of
fleshly desires, to be easily satisfied. He sighed, suddenly imprinted
on the mortal plain, turning away, secreting love through a world of
waiting hearts.*

The moment lasted forever. Otieno and Fiona shared their giggles with coffee and sloppy chips. As if counting freckles, or keeping each other's silence, holding it in. Agape love. Fiona laughed at the boy with almond eyes, Otieno winked at the girl with surprise in hers. Eros above them, weaving their future lives together.

'Ottie. this is another overly subjective account. The question asked for a critical appraisal of the literary text, not a pseudo-Greek Mythology-slash-documented love story, of your own imagination.'

April's Blue

Mira Schlosberg

April Abbotsleigh knew by the age of seven exactly what her favourite colour was, and where it was to be found. Her mother had a pair of sunglasses—cheap blue plastic things, badly beaten around the edges, that she had purchased in a train station in Italy. Before them she had had a pair of charcoal black frames, large and round and very expensive. They had been a present, from whom she couldn't recall anymore. She took them travelling with her. She was an archaeology student, had saved all her money to travel, and owned nothing nicer than those glasses. She saw Italy through them. Venice, Rome, cats asleep in sunny doorways, all tinted a few large round shades darker than real life. And then, on a train with a golden-brown interior, someone slipped the glasses from her handbag. She bought the new pair and three clichéd postcards in a souvenir shop inside a train station in Florence. And being a practical woman, and a believer in getting as much use as possible out of things before discarding them, she had the glasses ever since.

This was the story that accompanied the sunglasses that April's mother told again and again each time the subject arose. Stepping out of the shade, she would squint into the sunlight, unfold the thin plastic arms wearily, and sigh, saying, 'I had a lovely pair of sunglasses once.' It was years before April realised that her mother never really hated those blue Italian shades; she simply liked to talk about Italy, to remember a young woman with a pair of train station sunglasses and a lilac-coloured sundress billowing in the olive-scented air.

April, who knew nothing of Italy except that it was filled with old beautiful things and that everyone was glamorous (even the pickpockets) loved the glasses. She thought they made her mother look like a movie star, loved the way the chipped blue plastic looked with the deep plum colour of the lipstick she always wore. She idolised her mother in those glasses and was always asking to wear them. They were graded, split into three sections that faded, dark to light, down the lens of each eye. And it was in the middle section of these lenses, on days when the sky was perfectly blue, that April found her favourite colour. She would slip the glasses, too big for her at that age, onto her face and look up at the sky, and there it was, the same as always, her shade of blue. It existed in its own reality, in a world almost but not exactly like this one, a world framed by chipped blue plastic that faded dark to light, a few shades shadier than reality. It was an unreal colour, like the bleeding together of watercolour paints, like an old-fashioned hand-coloured film, tinged with lemon-yellow around the edges. Almost but not exactly a perfect sky blue.

April watched the sky. She stared up at it, studied it. She knew its every shade. She saw the way the light came down from it and made the world change colour. Inside her mother's glasses, each time the sky changed colour, a careful and elegant invisible hand pencilled in the world accordingly. April watched, and she waited, and when the sky was perfectly blue she put on her mother's glasses and looked at it. April came to live in shades of blue. She knew them all by heart, theme upon variation, and she understood and categorised each one with a depth and purpose uncanny in someone of her age. Had she taken up chess, or the violin, or even dance, she might have been a prodigy, but she kept the colours to herself, and the world inside her mother's blue Italian shades.

The blue of the glasses' frames themselves often appeared in the sky. It was there very early on summer mornings and late on winter afternoons, when the sun wasn't shining too brightly. April liked this. It was as if the sky was acknowledging her, showing that it knew she was there, watching and waiting, glasses in hand. Then there was the clear, watery blue that came just after dawn every morning. It was the same shade as the waves in the ocean as they stretched themselves thin, up up up, and turned a smooth, minty teal before breaking. Pink clouds floated like fish through it, and a few scattered stars still shone like bubbles. At night the sky was red-violet-blue. It was a vivid and fiery colour, despite being almost black, like coloured lights shining behind a rich dark cloth. It brought with it the soft, smoky darkness that wrapped itself like wool around trees and gates and people and filled the streets. Sometimes the sky burned blue like the inside of a flame and made her worry that the world might catch fire. It was a bright, beautiful shade, the colour of the evening primroses the size of fists that draped and shone among the dripping greenery beside the train tracks.

And once, when it rained in the summer, she looked out of the window and saw that the sky was almost lilac purple. It was the colour of the jacaranda trees that blossomed for four weeks a year with bright blue-purple flowers that fell from their glowing branches and carpeted the ground. It was a colour that slowed time, daubed thickly onto a canvas with careful passion. A dreamy, warm–cool, evening–morning, soft–deep shade. A November colour. Impressionist blue. And then, of course, there was that perfect sky blue. It came suddenly with the feeling that it would last forever. It was the colour of expectation. It smelled of apple blossoms and tasted like salade niçoise. And for April Abbotsleigh, aged seven, it meant one perfect thing. She put on her glasses and watched the colour of the sky darken slightly.

April couldn't remember exactly when it was her mother lost her favourite colour. She could only remember remembering it. Often the thought of it came back to her, suddenly but naturally. It was there in the morning on a crowded bus and in the daydreams that interrupted the writing of a shopping list. The memory of a cheap pair of sunglasses from Italy, and a childish loyalty to a shade of blue.

Someone had given her these earrings; she couldn't recall who. They were simple but perfect; two multifaceted sky blue stones dangling from thin silver wires. They had a comforting weight to them that she liked. She had worn them today with a flowered scarf and lipstick, mauve, not plum like her mother's, to a café for lunch. Seated outside under the shade of a wide green umbrella, she looked up smiling. The day, she thought, was comfortingly calm and ordinary. Every movement made had great purpose but mattered little. She brushed her hair behind her ear.

Her finger caught on her earring, knocked it into the glass of lemonade in front of her. And suddenly there it was. She stared for a long moment at the earring in the bottom of her glass. It's colour changed by the liquid around it, it had transformed into something she had not seen for years, something long lost. And yet, there it was. Unexpected, perfect, a moment tinged with lemon yellow around the edges. A miracle in a glass of lemonade. Almost but not exactly a perfect sky blue. One long moment later, April picked up her spoon, unused, and fished the earring out of her drink. She dried it carefully on a napkin and placed it back in her ear, still smiling.

Sandstones like Sepia

Marija Elektra Rodriguez

Although I've only known you for sixteen weeks, I will love you until I am dust.

I whispered the words in his ear and entwined his fingers with my own. They were marble, hard as stone, glacially cold. The ebony was seeping into his wrist, barely visible past the cuff of his military uniform. It could have been a stain of ink, but I knew it was nothing so benign. His blood was discoloring, turning black. His skin had taken on a pallid tone. There were hepatic speckles across his hands. He seemed so small in death, shrunken, surreal— as though an unnamed artist had carved him from stone and laid him out on crimson silk. Just a statue. An imitation of life. Not the real thing.

My eyes strayed to his face. The crop of auburn hair, so like my own, had dulled, turned tawny in the flickering candlelight of the church. I resisted the impulse to touch his cheek. The stiffness of his hand had shocked me, sending a brief ripple of alarm through my chest. The bones of his face seemed more prominent in death than they had in life. And in a day there would be nothing left of his flesh. He would be burned, like medical waste. Then the ashes would be sealed in our family sepulchre, dusting the bones of our ancestors, piled upon each other. The thin line of his lips, those eyelids sewed shut, they would all dissolve. I would never see those onyx orbs again. Gone.

And it was my fault that he was going in the ground.

In the confines of the church, my mother and her sisters raised their mourning wails. The sound reverberated off the walls and drowned everything in sorrow. It was our tradition, our ritual. Inhaling the scented air, I attempted to join in the half-chant, half-screaming song—but the sound choked in my throat and a heavy, raspy breath escaped my lips instead. It was an obligation to the dead, this hideous cacophony. It kept away the pollution attracted to bloodshed, or so the old widows had told me in my youth.

But I no longer believed such superstitions.

Wetness tickled my face. Tears chased each other down my ashen cheeks. In the golden reflection of the tabernacle my eyes were two violet drops in a sea of liquid crystal. The small chest glittered with jewels that pulsed in the inconstant candlelight.

I looked over his dark navy jacket, the crisp white collar blossoming out upon his neck. I placed his favorite knife in the coffin upon his chest. Then I felt around in my pocket for the smooth, cool metal object that was tickling my thigh through the thin fabric of my dress. His cigarette lighter. How he had loved that thing. Flicked the small, metal latch backward and forward to watch the blue-gold light reappear. Traced his fingers over the elaborate engraving in the metal. The baroque letter 'R'. His name had been Romano. Just another lazy Sunday afternoon in our small cottage on the side of the volcano, flicking the lighter and following me with his eyes. 'We've all lost a child. It will get better with time.'

A gnarled hand clutched my elbow—one of my aunties, veiled in black. Only the white flesh of her neck and cheeks broke through the flatness of the color. Gelatinous orbs looked at me with pity, laced with blame. Her lips were bloodless, her mouth moving in a soft monotone of comfort. She whispered that last word through her solicitous stare and glazed emerald eyes. Time. I had nothing but time. I was only twenty-eight.

'You can try again.'

Try what again?

Back at home, in the small cottage, I laid two plates on the kitchen table. He wasn't there. I placed the bitter almond biscuits on his red silk handkerchief. Filled his glass with the honey-spiced wine. Lit a small red candle in his honour. Inhaled the cinnamon smoke of the flame and sprinkled a sulfur crystal upon it. I watched as the honeycomb yellow powder melted into a drop of viscous red foam.

Il giorno della morte. The day of the dead. The only day I set the table for two. I no longer believed in the custom, but it felt wrong not to perform it.

I sat and flicked a cigarette lighter as he had done. It bathed the room in amber.

A crescent moon watched me from behind lace curtains. The patterns in the fabric created luminous figures that danced upon the cottage floor and across my toes. I could see the Doric temple from the window in my chamber. The remains of the Greek theatre and cemetery lay just to its side. They lit up the ruins at night. Sandstones, the color of sepia. The Christians had tried to build a church over the pagan site, but abandoned it when lava erupted and almost drowned the temple in flames. A sinewy, red-gold snake, flowing down the side of the volcano, the tear streaks from the ancient god trapped below the mountain. That volcano was littered with superstitions.

Snakes carry the souls of loved ones. The widows' words ricocheted in my mind. I could see the small silhouettes of the women as they left the honeyed cakes and bitter almonds for the serpents. *Take the sweet biscuits. Let me know he still lingers.*

But you will never be a snake. You will never be buried in the ground.

Just a few drops of blood. Maybe it's not so bad. Plenty of women bleed when they are pregnant.

But the acid in my gut and the red snake down my thigh tell me differently. My body has betrayed me. And your father, Raphael, had those long, rounded lashes—like spider legs shooting from his eyes. He is already in the ground, but you cannot go with him.

You are too little.

My mother drops her plate with honeyed cakes and bitter almonds. The spiced wine splashes the stone floor of the cottage. Mixes with the small red drops of you.

She starts to wail and her sisters join in. There is no church, no coffin.

There never was, and there never shall be.

Just the sandstone, sepia temple, with the ancient statue of the goddess in the middle. The one the Christians threw into the sea but that washed back to the black soil of the volcano. I would have named you Romano. And I can fit you in the palm of my hand.

Although I've only known you for sixteen weeks, I will love you until I am dust.

'We've all had miscarriages. It will get better with time. You can try again.' My aunty, the black-wrapped widow.

But you will never be.

In Extremis

Audrey Menezes

Still upon the beds they lay
Near lovers burdened by the
gloom
The dancing men of yesterday
As death and misery both loom.

Lo! How Chance reared its dark
head!
The merriment was seized with
haste
And slicing simply at the thread
It watched the frays of life,
displaced.

Now in shining halls of white
Time picks up its task from
Chance
As calmly it observes man's plight
But dares not fetch him in advance.

They wait and bide in mute unease
The kin with expectations sparse
Heads bowed, no deity to appease
No recourse yet at hand to parse.

Now Chance returns with silver blades
And Time retreats into the grey
To watch the rhythmic rough cascades
Of dancing men of yesterday.

Lucinda O'Brien

ARNA Artwork Intermission

Eleanor Gibson
Untitled (2012)

Nik Thorup
Benares (2012)

 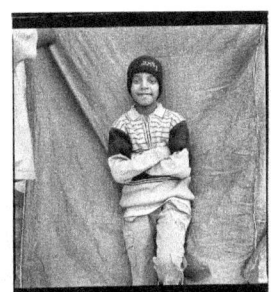

'I spent the last two months of the holidays living in the holy city of Varanasi - working on these photographs, reading, writing and playing frisbee by the Ganges. All of my pictures were shot on three different film cameras. I choose film as my medium because I feel it makes me a better photographer. I brought a digital camera with me on my last trip to India but found the results unrewarding and despised the fact I was spending too more time looking at a screen instead of looking at the world.

The photographs are a part of my "good-karma-photo-project". I have taken down the names, ages and occupations of all subjects (around 80 or so) and have promised to send prints back to them. I have yet to develop another forty or so pictures from this series. I basically wanted to capture the diversity of the city by photographing as many people as I could. Unfortunately not a lot of women in India are keen or allowed to get their photographs taken.'

Amelia Goldie
Submerge (2012)

Amelia Goldie

The Power of One (2010)

Amelia Goldie

Untitled (2010)

Kathryn Beaton
The Casualties (2012)

Kathryn's work explores a mind's living consciousness and its connection to the natural world, intertwined with contemporary issues relating to anxiety. Her works are composed of traditional etchings, screen prints, digital drawings and more recently film and animation. The familiar, natural and sentimental meet old, discarded and dead items to explore life as a more transient state. Honesty and exploration of the human condition is a strong undercurrent of Kathryn's work, due to her having lost two loved ones to brain cancer. The effect of the disease is explored in order to come to terms with loss and express a desire for further research into the illness. Images such as growing organic life intertwined with skeletal details are reminders of mortality, as fragile and exposed forms explore the inseparable nature of life and death.

Ania Gareeva
Les Irreguliers (2012)

'Most of my friends look at my drawings and paintings and say that they are "weird" and "strange", but at the same time quirky and whimsical. I guess that is what I try to achieve in my collages, drawings, watercolours, acrylic and oil paintings. Something different and unconventional, yet equally as beautiful and aesthetically captivating. Most of my artworks are enveloped by these somewhat antithetical characteristics; portraits of fancy dressed Victorian animals, mutated and eyeless original characters. I am a self-taught artist and continuously try to explore different mediums and develop and solidify my own original artistic style. In the past year or so, I have also been focusing on my Russian background and taking influences from Russian history and literature, thus my art is becoming a transmutation of my personal and cultural contexts.'

Joseph Turrin

Arctic Exploration 1-4-90 (2008)

Andrew Kim

Difficulties (2012)

'I don't exactly know myself what the problems are.
But I will overcome all the difficulties. One day. I think.'

I will overcome this night

Andrew Kim

I will overcome this rain

Andrew Kim

I will overcome this Sea.

Andrew Kim

Shaung Wu
Disembodied (2012)

The Chinaman's Garden

William Kilner

Our childhood playground, the Chinaman's Garden, was destroyed by the council one afternoon in June. It was a cold and blustery day in this quaint part of the Southern Hemisphere. We sat on our bikes, on top of a hill, looking down. We could see clearly, but it was some distance, about a kilometre. They looked like giant bees. But only one of the machines moved its limb—its limb—the other two were decommissioned, demobilised.

The Chinaman's Garden—what was it? Who was the mysterious Chinaman? Did he really exist? Or was he only a figment of Redcliff's imagination?

I looked over at Tim, who watched as the garden was torn apart. His appearance was serene; his lips relaxed, neutral. His eyes warm and indifferent. He was not shocked. I didn't know what he was. I knew it didn't mean as much to him. I felt something in me drop. A cord snapped. It was waking up to find that the dream you'd been having was only a dream. The single machine extended its long claw—its claw—pulling up a heap of debris. We couldn't see any people—workers, that is. The loader gave the strange impression of working itself.

In the several years leading up to its destruction, there were many stories that went circulating about the garden. Indeed, these were no doubt what led to its ultimate fate, as the garden had become notorious in Redcliff. Some of the stories stretched the imagination somewhat, with supernatural undertones, such as the story of Kyle Spatt. One day at Redcliff Primary a rumour went around that another kid had been inside the garden. His name was Kyle Spatt. He had gone into the garden the previous afternoon and

when he didn't come home for dinner his parents called the police.
He had been seen wandering, shirtless, or naked—depending on
which version—along Silverton Road, the road that went past the
western side of the garden. Cars going past honked their horns and
flashed their high beams. They said when the police picked him up
he was confused. He told them he was going to the supermarket,
but that was on the other side of the garden. Other versions
claimed that he was trying to get to the highway, that he was going
to hitchhike to Sydney...

'And what happened?'

'Well, he came back to school after a week. We saw him in the
playground at lunch. He looked normal, as far as normal goes.
But he was only back for a week and then he was gone again. One
version was that he had disappeared, abducted by aliens. Another
that his family had just moved to Queensland. I wanted to know,
so I asked the year five teacher, Mr Drake, one day, while he was on
playground duty.'

'What did he say?'

'He told me it was none of my business.'

Ten or so years later I moved to Sydney. I was living with my
girlfriend in the Inner West. It was she who suggested I try to write
a story about the garden. One morning we were at the breakfast
table. Sam was reading the paper. At twenty-five, we were already
veterans of domesticity. I was planning an afternoon bike ride
for us, so I had a map spread out before me. 'Some farmers are
protesting in the city today,' Sam said.

'What about?' I replied, without looking up from the map.

'There's a highway being built through their land,' she said. 'It's
like that film.'

I mumbled something. Sam went back to reading. I was looking
around the CBD area, and that's when I saw it. A little patch of
green in Darling Harbour. Chinaman's Garden. A gulp rose in
my throat. There were some other patches of green in the vicinity.
Hyde Park was to the northeast, a long vertical rectangle, and

Wentworth Park was to the northwest. The Chinaman's Garden was a small island in between them. The images I had associated with the garden as a child flashed in my mind. The bamboo wind chime hanging in the entrance of the hut. The bamboo grove, full of sunlight. Those were real. But the Chinaman's dark face, and the long pipe which hung from his mouth—the face that still returned in my dreams—where had that come from?

I must have looked shocked. 'What's wrong?' Sam asked.

I shrugged. 'There's a Chinaman's Garden in Sydney,' I said.

'Huh? What's that?'

'Nothing. There was a place called the Chinaman's Garden in Redcliff when I was a kid. That's all.'

'Oh, you mean the Chinese Garden?' she said.

'Chinese Garden?'

'At Darling Harbour. My dad used to take us there when we were kids. It's really nice. I can't believe you've never been there.'

I looked at the map again. She was right. It was 'Chinese Garden,' not 'Chinaman's Garden'. And yet that was what I had read. I stared at the words: 'Chinese Garden'. Had the word changed on the page, the universe playing with me, I wondered. Or had I simply seen what I wanted to see?

'What's wrong?' Sam asked me. 'You look concerned about something?'

'It's nothing,' I said, like they say in the films. But I didn't want to talk about it. I had only ever talked about it with Tim a couple of times long after it was gone. Apparently he had more or less forgotten it. I mentioned some of the stories that circulated about it back in the day and he only laughed. He entertained me, but I could tell he wasn't into talking about the subject. Maybe he sensed that it had taken another shape for me, some weird shape beyond what he cared to try to understand. It had been years now since I'd seen or spoken with Tim.

That afternoon we rode through St Peters, along the Princes Highway, and then along the Cooks River. In parts of the river that weren't concreted, I thought I saw some little fish. The water looked strangely clean and there were even mangrove remnants that we rode past. Sam smiled as we rode along. She looked like a goof in her helmet. I suppose I did, too. On the way back we stopped in a park and had some fruit, nuts and water from our bags. I had the map out, and was looking around the Inner West area. But my eyes kept going back to Darling Harbour.

'What are you looking at?' Sam asked.

'Just looking at the route we've taken,' I said, and bit into my pear.

'So what else happened in this garden you were talking about?'

I swallowed. Something rose in my throat again. 'Not much. They said kids did drugs in there, and that a girl was raped. A week later it was knocked down. But there were always different stories. Who knows what actually happened.' I had become secretive all of a sudden, without any reason to be so. My girlfriend was more than attentive, considerate, and above all willing to listen to all that I had to say. She would have listened, and she would have understood, had I been willing to tell her about it. But some part of me felt protective of the garden, as if now that there was this copy, I had to protect the original.

'Did you ever go in there?' Sam asked.

'Once. Tim and I did.'

'And?'

'Nothing, really,' I said, hesitating. But another part of me did want to discuss it. In fact, in some ways I probably needed to discuss it. And seeing that she might lose interest if I said nothing else, I went on. 'Except there was a tin shack, with a girl inside. There was a bamboo windchime hanging in the door. And behind the shack was like a bamboo grove and there was a kid in there with a big machete, hacking at the bamboo. He yelled out at us and we ran. He chased us for a while, but we got away. We had to cross a creek to get out on the other side and Tim fell in. His mum cracked the shits. He told her he'd fallen in a puddle but I think she knew we'd been in the garden. It was pretty notorious by that stage.'

'So you went into the garden after you had been forbidden?'
She smiled. 'And you could've been hacked to bits by a loon with a
machete.'

'It was kind of exciting, actually. You know, like *Fight Club*. A
brush with death.'

'That's what all kids want.'

'Exactly.'

I threw the pear core away at some trees. We got on our bikes
again for the ride back. The sun was going down, and everything
was quite was pleasant. We rode past tin fences, with bushes
hanging over them, along smooth, white concrete that had been
freshly laid. Cars went by on the highway, we smelt the somehow-
pleasant exhaust fumes. The sky went blue and pink. Sam was
riding ahead of me.

Once we were home and after we had dinner, a shower and
made love (shower and love simultaneous), I retreated into our
bedroom while Sam watched TV. I sat down on the sofa chair
and thought about the garden. I recalled one morning as we were
leaving Tim's house to go down to the skate bowl. 'Don't you boys
go into that garden,' Tim's mum had said. 'That Chinaman'll get
youse.'

I went into my drawer and got out my black book. I looked up
Tim's number and stared at the number for a while. Then I got the
phone off the desk and dialled. It rang three times and then picked
up. 'Hello.' Tim's voice was deep and gentle.

'Hello. It's Frank. How's it going?'

'Frank! Not bad. It's been ages, man. How are you? I'm just
getting ready to go out, actually.' We caught up. He told me about
his apprenticeship. I told him about my job with the magazine, and
Sam's job at the uni. Then he told me about his apprenticeship again
and I filled out some of the finer points about Sam's job. We talked
for ten minutes before the conversation wound to a still-point, and
I could tell he wanted to get off. But I kept him on the line. There
was an awkward pause. Tim cleared his throat. He was about to say
something to excuse himself.

The Chinaman's Garden | *William Kilner*

'Do you remember the Chinaman's Garden?' I asked him. I felt
stupid, but excited. It felt like we were back in a familiar situation,
which no doubt would reveal a familiar impasse. But it was this
impasse that I wanted to open up, and to break, even if it was
impossible. He remembered, he said. They knocked it down, and
there was a block of units there now. I asked if he remembered the
day we went in there. He laughed. He remembered, he said. Did he
remember the tin shack? And the girl inside smoking? He wasn't
sure it had been a girl, but he vaguely recalled a tin shack. I felt
triumphant. I didn't care that I sounded obsessive. 'By the way,' I
said. 'There's a Chinaman's Garden in Sydney. Well, it's a Chinese
Garden, actually. But it's kind of strange, don't you think, that there
should be two gardens?'

'So?' Tim said. 'What does that have to do with the price of eggs
in—'

'In China?' I asked. He had to go. He was going to be late.
I hung up the phone and sunk back into the chair. I could see
her eyes, languid, in my mind. The eyes radiating indifference,
boredom.

What was the Chinaman's Garden?

In bed Sam put her arm around me. Her reading light was still
on. I stared at the wall, at a line where shadow met light. I lay still.
I was grateful for her arm, and for her presence. I had an urge to
pour my heart out to her, and to thank her simply for being her.
Still looking at the wall, I told her I loved her. She smiled. She said
it back. All was good.

'Perhaps you could write a story about it,' she said.

'About what?'

'The Chinaman's Garden.'

'Maybe.' I backed up a little and nestled in closer to her. She
wrapped a leg around mine. 'But where would I start?'

'Start with the council knocking it down. With you and Tim
looking on as the big yellow Tonka trucks move in to destroy your
childhood playground. That seems like a good place.'

'It wasn't really a playground, but that sounds good. It was more like a dark jungle, but in the middle of suburbia.'

'So you could use it as a symbol for nature within suburbia or something like that.' We were silent for a few moments. I was thinking.

'What was the name of that film again? The one where they try to knock down his house and he takes them to the High Court? There was something on the news about that protest today. One of the farmers got arrested. It reminded me of it.'

'*The Castle*? How is it that you don't know that film?'

'I know it. I just couldn't remember the name.' Sam took her leg down and readjusted herself again. We shifted until we were comfortable once more, now with one of my legs over hers and her left arm pressed into my chest, snug.

'You're right,' I said. 'It's not a bad idea. I could use it as a symbol, of nature, the Garden of Eden, and the encroachment of civilisation.'

'Hmm ... I didn't really mean it like that. Besides, do you really think it can handle that? It wasn't exactly a paradise, was it? You said it was full of weeds.'

'Yes, but they were our weeds—our scrub! It was where the wild things went—and the council came in and knocked it down, the way that Europeans invaded this country and tried to dispossessed the Aborigines.' I rolled over, ruining the mutually arrived at calibration we had just achieved. But I was getting excited about the idea.

'I think that might be pushing it a bit far, Frank.'

'But that's what *The Castle* does! Substitute a house for a country, an airport for the British Empire. If they can do it...'

She stroked my head. 'Don't think so big. Start with the Chinaman. Who was he? Do you know?'

'Well, I don't know if he ever existed, that's the thing. I think they just called it that. The funny thing is, I still dream about him. I see him smoking a long pipe, his face is in shadow. But his eyes ... they're warm and almost benevolent.'

'That's sounds nice. Shall I turn off the light?' The light was turned out.

The next weekend, Sam suggested that we visit the Chinese Garden. I declined. I wasn't against the idea in itself, but I felt squeamish about going. She told me that I had to see the Jade Pavilion, and the Dragon's Wall.

'The Chinese consider jade to be the ultimate gem. It symbolises longevity.'

I like jade, but up to the writing of this story I still have not visited the Chinese Garden.

Scribbles for a Mandate

Andrej Trbojevic

I want to fuck the solar system
The lustrous milky way,
Ignominious stain in the limited
night sky
Saline, translucent
Will never know why
So I dive into the girl-next-door
fantasy
Jazz up the side-stepping
innuendo
Rile up the limitless
admonished libido
And free it to the concatenation
of chaos and order
Furrowed exhalation
Mountainous chest
Stamina and faith at their best,
Put to the test
Desolate and insatiable in their assiduity

Scribbles for a Mandate | *Andrej Trbojevic*

Fucked-up in twirling revelry
Zeus had an Oedipus complex
We're complex as fuck, impervious, reckless
'What you've got to impress us with?'
A frustrated soul
Ornate control
No better than dust particles in air
No worse than the holy blood-sweat carvings
Of poured space and
A nothing that bespeaks itself
Interstellar intimacy
Its numinous lack of clarity
Static in its joy
Knowing well that life is
An odd permutation
In the primordial hibernation
Of the dark.

Dolls

Brendan O'Shea

To make something in one's own image is a highly biblical concept. The idea first came to me on a rainy night in the middle of summer, sometime after dinner in those late hours on the cusp of midnight. It's amazing what can happen in those hours; the student actually finishes the assignment due in a mere ten hours time and a genius might realise the nature of the universe while washing the dishes. What happened that night was just as mundane as understanding the universe while washing dishes. There was an episode on the TV, I'm not sure of the series but it was definitely something Japanese, where a sentiment was expressed in words by a fictional character better than I can. 'Mankind creates dolls in her own image.' Perhaps we're all a collection of dolls.

I looked into the thin sliver of a mirror and saw my face for the first time. It was a pale face, glinting in the low light like porcelain but soft like human skin. It felt unreal to touch my own skin and not feel the warmth. I'm not sure how I would even begin to describe the sensation of feeling nothing; there's nothing like it. Maybe that's a good thing, that humans could feel things. Placing the mirror back on the metal gurney beside me, I wasn't sure exactly how it was that I felt about losing touch.

My choice to undergo the process wasn't just the decision of a giddy idiot. There was still legal tape to work through and preparations to be done. It's almost as if I was being drafted into some kind of army, except instead of psychological assessments and physical tests I was meticulously examined to determine the exact sizes of my body parts. The doctor had looked just a little bit too pleased as he wrote down the measurements of my shin, thighs and arms.

'You are sure you want this design?'

He coughed while I thought it through. Did I actually want to go through the process? I tried not to shake my head as images of bloodied scalpels and the smell of anaesthetic flooded my mind. I nodded. The doctor smiled; I must have looked slightly sick. That was all over. I was a jigsaw person held together by thin wire. The doctor had certainly known what he was doing. I'd seen friends pass from flesh to plastic with blood still covering their hands like some sort of webbed glove. My hand was clean and perfect. There was no blood I could see. A smile tried to force itself across my face, but there's only so little you can express with a plastic mask; complete neutrality. I remembered the reflection in the mirror. The face that had stared back was a gothic and unfamiliar sight with no smile. That was my face.

The outside world seemed different. Night air just doesn't have the same chill to it when you can't feel the cold. Rain fell down on me and I couldn't feel the drops running down my face or through my hair, through the black wig on my head. I could still smell the fresh smell of rain and I could remember the rain as I had known it. There had been days where I would run through the grass and feel the mud oozing through my toes and it was blissful. The rain would fall onto my outstretched tongue and I stared into the dark sky with wonder, curious why the sky seemed to cry. It was the sort of story I had wanted told at my bedside, but I was told something about evaporation and precipitation; nothing as magical as I had imagined. My feet passed through the mud and I couldn't feel it through my toes. I kept on walking.

'Come now and receive your free Processing!' the ads had said with their little cartoon man waving from out of the screen with an idiot grin you just wanted to punch. Have you ever wanted to punch one of those people in the face just to stop the TV ad? 'Live with a body that can never age; live with the body that you want for yourself!'

I remember when the news stations latched onto stories of suicides. The notes were always the same. 'I don't know who I am anymore' was the most common. My face was a shock, yes, but I knew I was still me. Besides, I chose to do this. I wasn't forced into this by anyone else. This was entirely my decision, so I wasn't sure why my mind immediately went to the suicides. I could live without the mud through my toes and the rain on my tongue. It was a small price to pay if it meant I would never age again.

*　　*　　*

I'm not sure if God's a benevolent toymaker like Geppetto or some malevolent puppeteer pulling our strings in some danse macabre, but it's an interesting thought that to create dolls in the image of mankind humans have essentially becomes gods themselves. Even a writer is somewhat godlike in the way they too carve and create characters in the image of themselves, with some even being omniscient guides granting the mere illusion of free will as they push the characters towards their own demise. The toymaker however has never been able to do anything like that. As they stare back at the static plastic face, or polished wood or even fragile porcelain, the toymaker realises they only have an empty shell for their troubles. The hours of careful craftsmanship leave nothing but a statue, a lidless statue staring out with hauntingly real eyes. It's a highly unsettling experience to say the least, watching over your back just to make sure the doll hadn't moved. Once I thought I saw one raise its arm, but I'm not sure if it was just my imagination. Perhaps everything is.

Even if it is a biblical concept it's very human to try and create life, isn't it? Perhaps it's something about mankind reaching its full potential, creating an entirely new life. Maybe it's simply curiosity, people simply wishing to know a little bit more about themselves and how they came to be. There's no way to create life, though, without trying to understand life first. Many men have sat before an apple at a table and questioned how they could prove the apple was alive; each wasted away into a brittle husk with the work of their life nothing more than ink on paper. I'm not quite sure what happened next. As always one thing probably led on to another, drawings and stories to my daughter of a night-time turning ever gradually into designs and detailed analyses throughout the waning hours of the moon. I didn't do any of the moulding myself, but I signed at door when the boxes from China arrived and oversaw the careful placing of organs and veins within the plastic shell.

*   *   *

I had never woken before and been completely wet. It was the morning dew that used to lie on everything, even the smallest blade of grass. I can still remember that, the sight of dew on the grass. It feels so long since I'd last seen it. I guess that's part of what being a human was all about; seeing things change and not even realising how your mind was changing until it was too late. When had I last even bothered to look and see the morning dew on the grass? It had been when I was a child, when I still had a mind that was addicted to wonder.

Stepping out of the hole I'd been sleeping in, I noticed I was near a small forest. The green was gone. There were just skeleton trees there; black and emaciated, branches stretching feebly up to the sky as if hoping that God or Mickey Mouse or the Cheshire Cat would save them from a bushfire. I couldn't feel the tears on my face as they flowed, but I could feel them in my eyes. It was strange how the most crucial part of a human, the most fragile and delicate of them all, had been one of the only parts that hadn't been replaced with plastic or glass. Had they gotten lazy? I really didn't care. It was comforting to know that I could still cry. Even if we were perfect, with all the plastic and careful moulding and couldn't bleed, tears could still fall from our eyes. *My God*, I thought to myself, *I can't bleed*. It was such a simple thought, but it still hadn't quite hit me yet until then. I couldn't bleed.

'Its post-op shock,' said a voice, old and wheezy like the breeze. Slowly I turned around to see a doll, clothes marred with mud and a jagged crack fracturing his face. I just nodded and wiped the tears from my face. The doll walked over, closer, his feet scraping through the ash. I began to stand up, carefully dusting the ash off my dress. When I looked towards the doll again his hand was outstretched; I looped my plastic fingers over his battered hand and it was then that I felt it. I could feel the pull in my muscles as he pulled me closer to himself and the strain in my legs as I began to walk.

'Do you still feel anything?' I asked as the trees began to grow sparser. 'Muscles, tears, pain...?'

'There is nothing left,' the doll said. I wasn't sure if I was stretching to try and hear pain or regret in his voice, because he didn't change pace or say anything more until forest was gone and I stopped, staring at the ground. There was something peering through the ash that I hadn't thought even existed. A small blade of grass had grown through the ash, a single glint of colour in the blackness. For a brief moment I could feel long grass whipping against my outstretched hands, but it was fleeting. In a kick of ash the blade vanished. The doll pulled me along.

*   *   *

When the sun crept through the barred windows and the workers fell asleep by the air con I would still be holding her blank face. The plastic was smooth, uncannily soft but lacking human warmth. No matter how beautiful or life-like the geisha-face in my hands was, it was still nothing more than a mask. There wasn't any blood flowing beneath the skin or a faint blush in her cheeks. She was cold plastic. Is that the truth of human cexistence? Not before, but after everything's over, do we turn into old shells of who we were?

Maybe there was more to my project than just satisfying my own curiosity, perhaps there was something that a greater person than me could find in the papers strewn throughout the warehouse and develop that could benefit humanity. I remember watching as that mask was lowered onto her head and the final stitching was done to sew together the monstrous beauty made by my Frankenstein-like hand. Her eyes flickered like a child's as she took her first look into the world. Stroking her cheek, now warm against my hand, I wondered for a moment if this was what it was like for a mother holding her newborn child in her arms. All I knew as I looked into her deep brown eyes was that I had created her and she was beautiful.

*   *   *

It had happened so quickly that I still wasn't sure how it happened. When he was in the throes of violence I don't even recall what I was remembering at the time. Perhaps it had been how kindly he'd seemed when we met in that forest, offering me a hand when I wasn't sure it was possible, that was distracting me at the time. That was past. Staring at the unfamiliar face peering out at me from the water, I tried to sniffle or cry or even just howl in agony. It was impossible. There was no agony, no reason to cry. There was just an eye hanging through its shattered socket by the thinnest of human threads.

'You think you're a pretty one, don't you?'

Those were the words he said before he kicked me to the ground. That was the only memory I had of it; being kicked to the ground. *Is this the result of everything*? It was the question that resounded in my head as I washed my face. Trying to avoid pain, improve beauty and destroy the problem of age forever; wasn't that noble? As I tried to place my eye back into my face I knew only one thing, that nothing had killed jealousy. It didn't fit. I tore it out, gasping as the thread snapped and the ball of jelly exploded over my hand. I assume it was cold. I splashed the water around; cleaning my hand of most of what had been my left eye. It was my eye no more.

I sat down by the bank for a long while; I didn't know if it was a river or just a creek. Time passed by, but it was impossible to tell with the cloud cover choking the sky. I remembered seeing paintings of a sky bright blue and the sun beaming on the green grass below, but it was an age ago, before this world of plastic and humans so powerful they could actually create new bodies for themselves. For us, I amended as I stared into my own plastic palms. There was still some eye-jelly covering my left thumb. I curled my hand into a fist, holding back the tears leaking from my single eye. My fist pummelled against the mud of the riverbank. I stood up on wobbly legs, flexing my fingers and staring at the strange, glossy earth clinging to them. Howling, I kicked at the water and then tore up the earth. I fell into the soft mud and sobbed into my hands, lying there like a wounded animal.

I'm not sure when I tore myself out of the mud. To my surprise, the world didn't look so different with only a single eye. It felt as if I was missing something, as if tearing out my eye was supposed to make things look different and half the world should have vanished from my gaze. Everything remained. Hobbling along, I walked through the everything that still surrounded me, a faint fog slinking along the ground. Ahead there seemed to be a house, tucked away in a pocket of the fog and only visible due to the dark blue door that stood as if solitary in the whiteness. Stepping over rock and twig, pulling my feet through the swamp of mud, I moved towards the house. I could hear the sharp calls of something. I thought it was a bird of some kind, but I knew I was imagining things. I had to be imagining things.

Placing my hands on the wet window by the door I peered into the house. There was a clock, tall and hewn from wood, standing in the corner ticking away even after it had so obviously been abandoned. A painting of a man rising from the earth hung just beside it, positioned as a portrait. The wallpaper was peeling at the edges, revealing a white wall behind the dull green that was chipped and scarred. I ran my hand over the empty socket and looked into the house more intently. There, on a table pushed next to the right-side wall, was a photo frame. I could feel a tear begin to fall from the only eye that I had left as I saw that photo.

There were three figures, a grey-haired man with little spectacles teetering on his Roman nose and a child much like him with freckles and blonde hair that would have been a radiant gold in life. I knew that better than anyone. Standing alongside them was a doll, standing tall and draped in a black dress much like the one that I was then wearing. The wig on her head, a raven black, was the same as the one I was wearing. Looking at that doll, at her face, I could see why that man had sacrificed so much. She was a plastic goddess, the final result of everything carved or moulded that had come before her. Looking at that beautiful face one last time, I realised exactly what I had sacrificed. Falling away from the door, my knees buckling, I wept into plastic hands, hands that had until so recently been flesh and blood. Those hands had once played with dolls of their own, hands that had torn the eye that first lay eyes on dolls and conspired to turn me into this plastic creature. It was the final result of everything. It had always been inevitable.

In the Kitchen

Carolina Skibinski

I thought I could gnaw my way
to the floor,
From the stove on which I sat
down.
But I found that my teeth,
Were not stone,
But the guards of a whistling
sound.

Edit

Carolina Skibinski

Help me edit the meat,
Clay's all I need.
We'll fill in the bricks with peat,
ash and seeds.
Flowers will bloom,
In the moisture between.

A Portrait of Ena Markovic

Carolina Skibinski

She walks down Harrow Lane,
and at a bend pauses to bloom.
A tall, tall window frames her.
She spins to draw the curtain
and reveals a vine pregnant with
flowers.

We see the full moon, and she
says, imagine if sanctuary shone
through that circular eye.
To halve our desk, we reify a
line of symmetry. We face one
another across the surface of a
pond.

Ants

Adam Chalmers

Sarah woke up gasping for air. She'd been having the most peculiar dream. Its details were already slipping her mind, leaving nothing but a vague sense of unease. Something about... animals? Bugs? Whatever they were, they had several more legs than she.

Bristling faintly at this injustice, Sarah hit her still-ringing alarm and ran to the shower. Its warm jets washed away both the sweat and unease left by the dream. She emerged clear-headed, the dream forgotten.

Sunlight streamed over her suburban garden and through the kitchen window as Sarah prepared breakfast. She stuck two pieces of bread in the toaster, and grabbed a jar of jam from the fridge, ready to twist it open, when—

'Eww! Ants!' she yelled. Indeed, making their way through the jar's contents were a dozen or so tiny black ants. 'Mum! The jam's full of ants!' No answer. Her mum must still be asleep. Never mind. Sarah threw the jar into the bin, and went back to the fridge. Ants were crawling around the purple encrusted circle left behind by the jam jar. It looked like they'd made it into the Vegemite as well. Sighing, she threw away the other ant-ridden spreads. Ah well. She'd just make an omelette instead.

The fridge was flung open again, and Sarah grabbed two eggs as the frying pan heated on the stove. She cracked them against the bench top and broke the first egg over the frying pan. But instead of a dripping pillar of eggwhites, a flailing stream of ants poured out.

Sarah screamed and dropped the egg. Its flimsy shell shattered, revealing more ants. How did this happen? Why was her egg filled with ants? How did they get there?

As if in answer to her question, the other egg cracked open too, its shell fracturing under the pressure of a thousand ants pushing outwards. She screamed again, her voice equal parts terror and confusion. An awful sizzle reached her ears, and she looked down. The ants from the first egg were burning on the hot frying pan. She watched in horror as they squirmed over it, searching for escape as they were slowly cooked.

She panicked and reached for the tap. She aimed it at the ant-covered eggshell on the bench top and squeezed the nozzle. But instead of delivering its high-pressure jet of water, all it delivered was a high-pressure jet of ants.

The ants shot out of the tap and rebounded against the hard marble counter, spraying all over the kitchen. Other ants continued to pour out of the two eggshells, and were slowly making sense of their new environment. When they'd left their eggshell, they had been an unorganised mass of insects. But now they were forming orderly lines and crawling off the counter and across the floor towards her.

'Mum! Mum!' Sarah cried as she backed away from the ants. 'Mum! Ants! Everywhere!'

'Sweetie? Are you alright?' her mum's voice echoed throughout the house. It was weary, still carrying the midnight cobwebs of sleep, but a note of alarm was beginning to tear them away. 'Is everything okay? I'm coming down now.'

'Come quickly!' Sarah screamed. She grabbed the phone off the wall and dialled her dad's mobile. 'Dad? Dad?' Sarah sobbed into the phone as he picked up. 'The ants ... they're everywhere ... they're coming closer!' The ants had covered the marble counter and had started to spread out across the floor.

'Dad? Dad!' she yelled, but no one replied. Instead, the quiet hum of the phone line was broken by a dull scratching noise, the faint sound of something brushing against plastic. Her eyes widened with terror as she slowly pulled the phone from her ear and looked into plastic grill covering the speaker. Something ... something was moving inside it. As she watched in disbelief, a slow trickle of ants began to climb out of the phone.

The sound of a thousand tiny ant-legs moving in unison was broken by her mother's bounding steps down the hall. 'Sarah? What's going on?'

'Mum!' Sarah ran to her mother and collapsed in her arms. 'The ants … they came from everywhere … I don't know how this is happening! We need to get out of the house!'

'Shhh, shhh, shhh. It's going to be okay. Just breathe. Everything's fine.' Her mother cradled Sarah to her chest and hugged her tight. 'We're going to be just fine.'

'But Mum, the ants are everywhere! We've got to get out of here,' she protested.

'Hush now, Sarah. It's fine. What are you worried about? Ants are harmless. Ants never hurt anyone. The ants are our friends.'

An icicle of fear stabbed its way deep into Sarah's heart. 'Mum … are you …' the words trailed off as her mouth suddenly closed. A lone ant crawled across her mum's face.

'Shhh. Everything's going to be okay,' her mum said, in a dead, monotonous voice.

'Oh no. No. No! They've gotten to you too!' Sarah screamed and pushed her mum away, escaping the maternal embrace. The older woman started and her eyes widened in surprise as she lost her balance and fell. Her mother crumpled as she hit the floor, and as each limb thudded into the hardwood, it disintegrated into a mass of insects. Like a sandcastle hit by a soccer ball, her mother's body decomposed over the course of a second into its millions of constituent ants.

The ants swarmed over her mother's clothing. '*Join us*,' they seemed to whisper with their tiny chittering mouths.

'Never!' Sarah screamed as she ran towards the door. Ants were still pouring out of the phone as it hung from the wall. The now million-strong swarm of ants was slowly spreading across the floor of the house, roiling in its shiny blackness.

Sarah fumbled with her keys as she reached for the doorknob. But instead of grasping its cold metal solidness, her hand plunged through the doorknob, which disintegrated into another disguised mass of ants.

'No!' The ants were crawling all over her hand. Panicking, she blindly swung her hand against the wall. Once. Twice. Three times. The ants were crushed, or thrown away by the force. Ignoring both her pain and the last few ants, she backed up a few paces and ran against the door, savagely battering it with her shoulder. The door flew open and she ran out of the house, the swarm of ants following behind her. She sprinted towards her car, eyes filling with tears of fright as she pulled the door open, scrambled in, and locked it. She turned the ignition and the car sprung to life with a reassuring growl. Flooring the accelerator, Sarah was pushed back as the car roared and shot down the street, leaving the house of ants far, far behind.

Looking back in fear to make sure she wasn't being followed, Sarah allowed herself a moment of relief. The road was long and straight, and the ants had been left far behind her. She flicked on the radio as she sped down the Pacific Highway's welcoming stretches of asphalt. Only static came from the radio. Her brow furrowed. Strange. Triple J must be down. She hit the button for preset two. Again, only static. With a terrible feeling of dread she pressed the third, fourth and fifth buttons, but nothing. Nothing except static. She looked down, and, as she knew was inevitable, saw a dozen ants slowly crawling out of the radio's speaker vents.

Something in her broke. She screamed again in terrible fear. The steering wheel dissolved into ants beneath her grip. More ants poured through the radio. The glove compartment burst open under the pressure of a thousand ants. The ants crawled out through the airconditioner vents and crawled towards her. She slammed on the brakes and reached for the door, but it wouldn't open. The light grew dim as ants covered the windscreen and windows. She was still yelling, but the ants had used this opportunity to crawl into her mouth. Gagging in fear and pain she buckled over as her vision went black and—

Sarah woke up gasping for air. She'd been having the most peculiar dream. Its details were already slipping her mind, leaving nothing but a vague sense of unease. Something about ... animals? Bugs? Whatever they were, they had several more legs than she.

Her limbs flailed within the white bed sheets as an orderly ran over to help her up. This wasn't her bedroom. Where was she? Everything was white, like some sort of hospital. The orderly wiped sweat from her brow and took a clipboard from her bedside table.

'Sarah Browning?' he said, his brown eyes examining the monitor above her bed. She looked back, too shocked for words.

'Welcome back. You've been unconscious for a few days now. You seem to have sustained some kind of stress attack midway through your exam period, and became delirious. We think you've had a fever of some sort, which broke a few hours ago. It's good to see you awake again.'

She looked around, taking in the new surroundings as the sound of rain falling on the rooftop rolled around her. It all came flooding back to her—the biology exams, the endless weeks spent hunched over insect anatomy diagrams and branches of the evolutionary tree ...

'Oh, uh ... thank you. It's good to be awake,' she said slowly, brushing sleep from her eyes and struggling to sit up in her bed.

'Just take it easy. We're going to keep you here for a few more days while you get your strength back,' he spoke over the rainfall. 'Could I just get you to sign this form?'

She took the pen from his hands, and they sat without talking while she filled in her details and wrote her signature. 'Nice bout of rain we've got,' she offered, as the sound of drops hitting the roof kept its steady pitter-patter.

He looked back at her and put his hand on her brow. 'It's ... it's not raining,' he said, pointing to the golden sunlight streaming through the open window.

She froze in fear. 'Then ... what's that sound?' she said, as both slowly raised their eyes to the rooftop, their gaze filling with dread.

The pitter-patter took a more ominous overtone. The roof began to shake. Little chips of white plaster fell down and crumbled. And then the roof fell in under the weight of a seething ocean of ants. Billions, trillions—no, far more. The walls disintegrated into ants, the table disintegrated into ants—the bed, floor and heart monitor all dissolved into ants, and Sarah and the orderly were left clinging to each other in terror as the world went black around them—

Villain

Ashley Hutchison

People often underestimate the value of some good honest villainy. Sometimes—just sometimes—you want to be the bastard who kicks the puppy, who steals the candy from the baby, who kinda-almost-nearly enslaves all of mankind. This is a feeling that strikes even the most virtuous of us at some point or another.

I would make a marvellous villain. Part of me thinks it's because I wholeheartedly embrace the necessity of a billowing black cape. But I think there are other, far baser, reasons for my aptitude in this profession.

There's my genuine disdain towards humanity. Most of them should die.

Then there's my sparkling wit for those gritty back-and-forths between my arch-nemesis and I.

And to top it off, I've an IQ which sits squarely in between Ted Bundy's and Jack the Ripper's (serial killers tend to be cleverer than most, I've read).

Oh, to be maleficent.

Untitled

Lucy Goldstein

A sweaty moon face drips its clean white light into the night, making visible the thin veins that pump purple paint underneath my skin. While I'm asleep they draw a map across my face, elaborate: mountains and ridges, seas and oceans, freckles that you thought sweet are tragic moons stuck in orbit, high cheekbones; tectonic plates that shift and collide between smiles and a grinding jaw. A mark beneath the brow, a hiding spot for broken Viking ships, buried rotting wood, reminders of raids that came in the night to burn down eyelashes and cast a shadow across the face. A desert in the south, thirty-two prickly pears grip their roots and hold against the wind; a proficient grin to puncture silence. Freckles pull the tides of saliva and the river mouth bleeds dry. Beyond paper edges, seawater rises, trout smack their tails against salty land and seven thousand intoxicated sea lice gnaw through electrical wires in the ear canal. Water un-writes ink and now knotted twists of hair are sailors' fallen anchors, drifting in the open. Mornings murder moons, milk and instant coffee and my same ceramic cup, the sunlight making visible your greaseproof-paper thin skin, the stubble on your face maps time, each tiny hair a gravestone for the days you couldn't bring yourself to dress.

For the First Time My House Has Music in It

Dashiell Moore

C to see and B to be,
Notes obtain the black
Running past the track
Music fingers see.

For the first time my house
—The floors that I crept on,
The ceilings that caught
Me singing or weeping

Has music in it
Restless beat to it, has people
besotted
Like a lawyer swears,
Hand on the first
To find a silent law
And have it curse.

They've lost a voice since I went
To foggy fields and far away
Exiled and blocked and sealed
Swallowed up and left behind
To mounds of memory
As far as eyes can see.

Arriving back to hear the din
Of dreaded calls
Slumped in gin.
The niche in stupor
It saw it all,
The spoken fist the slamming door.
The Leaving, the Terror, those Left.

The screech of harpies
Baying for blood from loved ones
You'd wake to hear the dead walk,
And hope it was the living that sing.

So now instead of left and last,
The past panelling forgets the she,
And the he, the dead singing soul songs
Can sleep amidst a cacophony.

For the First Time | *Dashiell Moore*

Whose fingers tinkle in hell,
Whose voice procures the bell?
I opened the door that first shut me
In and cast my eyes to tides of sea
To view a child, who sings of keys
To locked and empty things, to open
The heart of those who lost and still live
But wander if they might be found, for

Music makes flirtation love
A race to usurp the lake's drowning glove
Hands over heart or round a shoulder
Music can become a feeling that is written
And recorded, the pen's great gloating smile
Over dancing corpses of fathers
Who discover
A sighing time of dying, the lovely time of trying
To harass the music to rhythm, moving scrying
Dreams through the silent laws we wrote.

I can sleep now.
I dream of ivory and pain is illusory.

Avion

Dover Dubosarsky

Avion Brinly, a shoe shiner and eyelash trimmer, alone in the
world for no reason. A total horticulturalist and an incomplete
branch severer, he never gave in. He counted every raisin he was
given, neither forwards nor backwards, in a very similar fashion to
enumerating the pages in the Book of Sand. Evidence that he lived
life not to the end, but to swim.

Today was precisely the same as any other day. He woke up
vaguely early, somewhere in-between four or five. He required no
alarm as he naturally found himself awake. Avion shut the final
window, not giving the slightest chance for nature to expunge its
sunshine. Now in the bathroom he felt a requirement to live, so he
sat and stared from the toilet to the wall. A crack narrowed down
from the stained whitewashed tiles peering into his bellowed living
room. Perhaps being used as a spying tool, if he had any company,
or a short cut, if he could lose ninety-seven point sixty-two per cent
of his body mass.

After dressing and eating he rushed to Tempe Station and
caught a train to Central. He had nothing to do at home; it
simply provided a safe house for his restful nights and a storage
system for his worthless belongings. The train ride was short and
disheartening. A simple seat would have provided a sense of relief,
however the number of bags and the worry of touching minimised
the allocated seats. His short dark hair would allow simple
manoeuvring through tight spots and the sleeping masses. He in no
way attempted to foul the eyes of the common man with his own,
it just so happened that their unfortunately placed position and his
coincidently placed eyes sometimes caused a cataclysmic collision.

He arrived at Central neither a quarter past nor a quarter
late, but thirty-three minutes on the dot. There he set up shop

next to the newsstand, to serve the immaculate middle class. A rag and a jar of black shoe shine his tools. With gusto and strong hermeneutics he brushed, sub-atomically working, along the lines of a turntable, crossing both backward and simultaneously.

'Excuse me columnist, the *Times* seems to have *Mirror*ed the *Herald*'s calling. Did he not receive the *Telegraph*? Why has it not heard the *Bugle*'s blow?' Avion exalted at the miserable newsagent.

Avion was obsessed with the inclusion of tabloid publications. A distant disdain given to the existence of such garbage, yet the grouping of trash and its can caused a new synonym. Whilst language is defined by the people, if the people are stupid then should its basis also fall with it? English seems to fall in the former definition of tabloid. It can be viewed poorly for the purposes it is used: America a fat greasy state and Australia a land of uncivilised prisoners.

'What obscure theogony are you retorting? Have you swallowed a chimera?' came the usual stale response from the underwhelmed dictionary.

Avion would always orthogonally evict thoughts he deemed 'culturally unsound'. Riveting the garters would, in his opinion, place him at a thoughtfully rounded noontime prime. He sung to the visions in his mind, allowing them to flee gracefully. A soulless junkie walks by, a violin in one limb, and a broken bow in the other. If only you could walk towards the sound instead of against it. The armless visionaries and the doubtless horsemen, parading in the street, evading the complicated summations: to exhibit such a pastime, to abandon such a life, to restrict such a boundary.

'My lifeless world, give up your land, your seas, your power, but for heaven's sake not your doorways!' Avion shouted at the man, showing nothing but discontent for the penniless migrant.

The man stared, but didn't look. He watched but avoided acknowledgement. It wasn't for lack of eyes or for his already existing schedule, but instead to show lavishness. How does one live and not take? Or bake the cake and eat it too?

'To whom do you direct your consulate? Too many passers-by? Two times as many as the Moroccan chivalry guild I hear,' the vagrant mocked in a convenient manner.

Avion quickly responded, 'For the king's manner, my dear avarice. I worship the ground you seat and all you respond with is a slick excretion. Exit my vicinity or the dust shall shatter along your path.'

It wasn't every day of the week that Avion found himself in such situations. A disgruntled nod is shared between the two syndicates. A well-organised acceptance.

The rest of Avion's day can be summarised as the leaves of a small oak tree washing into the river, not a true cleansing of malnutrition but a mere frustration being simmered in the disdain of the past. He blanketed his belongings back into his tattered bag, with a loose knot, and then with a sturdy hoist over his back, he was ready to continue on his way.

Amble

Giacomo Bianchino

The last of the evening through sycamores crept
And gathered in pools on the banks where he stepped
As healthy indifferent the solar descended
There came a young stream where his footstep-path ended

As smiling, the terrible darkness fell softly
His spirits were murky, his sentiment lofty
A flashing eye turned to the firmament's gaze
He felt he had come to the end of his days

Those steps in the grasses and overturned stones
Were once somewhat lighter, he was not alone
For then, by his side did another one follow
The tilt of his joy, now the source of his sorrow

Without sweet romance, there's only the grave
And to the pale maggots, the emperor is slave
He sought not at all for the vague explanations
That adorn both the Holy and profane invitations

If all matters corporal measure for aught
As time and again, he had strictly been taught
Then surely, importance must certainly lie
In the purest of loves; and in nothing besides

All this thought the trav'ler, and made valid cases
Though erstwhile, in madness he conferred with faces
Conceived in the boughs of the sentinel trees
'Twas they alone who did temper his pleas

Idleness grows where the will remains weak
In indolent ears does the Fallen One speak
And so, as his consciousness seemed to unravel
An awful intention comported his travels

When love's first retainer took her selfish leave
He felt as a tapestry, coming unweaved
I then was a man, he thought 'pon reflection
Yet now all he was, was a thousand directions

Finally, fortune found our fickle mourner
Stayed at the edge of crag, found him cornered
The precipice searching, an end to discover;
All he discerned was the face of his lover

Amble | *Giacomo Bianchino*

Anxious is fear when we fear not a thing
But our own strange desire to solemnly fling
Ourselves from the edge of insensible fissure
And into the truths of our vague superstition

Before him arose the imminent fall
And hearkened he to its most harrowing call
Though, furtively searching, he could not begin
To tell if the voice did not come from within

Against the sheer face, he became silhouette
No longer a being of joy or regret
But an idling nothingness, limbo with form
Within him had ceased the furious storm

Compelled into action, our trav'ler stepped forward
No longer could suffer 'neath Damocles' Sword
Yet, 'pon the formation of vicious resolve
His quiet conviction did seem to dissolve

As he had made to steal from the edge
He felt himself pulled from the terrible ledge
Turning, the impudent saviour sought he
And saw nothing but evening creep through the trees.

Quay

Kate Farrell

Hairish grains, frozen grey,
sprung from soil now coarsely
timbered
and haggard hot, the sea's
retainer
is foot-faced and food
splattered
astride the mumbling waters.
Boardwalk of circuses
parading patrons
for the feather-blue hollow sky,
who inspects
today's haul; cash-breathed
Americans, fat,
fished 'neath empty ether.

Public servant exemplary, tree-carcass biding
years, weathering salt and dirt and worn
thoughtlessly like underwear,
bearing believers in topaz pendants
oriented MCA-ward amid

Quay| *Kate Farrell*

bubble-gum tourists
talking Self and tacky ornamented
thoughts be-thunk
in bubbles taut,
burger orders spoken solemn
sticky with aplomb.
Scored across
old plank and post, that moving
tattoo of ephemera.

Wooden host and watcher
wound in blasé tramping tides, purveyor
crumbed in careless coin,
soled flat and sailed by breeze-borne
blousey articles of art—caught
fast and trapped in flaccid furrows
this crown of crinkly litter-people
filleted alive, atop, ashore the
supine warf
shod deep and darkly wet
in harbour manga
dozing.

Wooden Duck

Mariana Podesta-Diverio

Symbols of strength
gather dust as they
sit on shelves
initially carefully
placed aside
becoming heavier with
age
undisturbed specks
groups of sixty ticking past
symbols lasting
trials other elements cannot
attempts to brush dust
off elements fall
alongside strength symbolised
preserved perseverance
perspiring, pathetically
placed alongside
symbols of strength
on shelves
leaving pockmarked
layers, dusty

strength symbol-shaped outlines of
puzzle pieces atop
cedar.
Landscaping fondant
partitions radiating
mumbled affirmations
cliché
marked collocations
fixed collocations
inadequate consolation
trying matters the most
hosting feelings
sentiment well-intended
sentient
open-ended invitation
restrain from overcompensating
pinching dust through barren
fingertips feels
substance isn't
fast forgotten—
pockmarks linger.

WHEN TWO PERCENT WERE STUDENTS

Gorgeous expansion of life
all day at the university,
then home to be late for meals,
an impractical, unwanted boarder.

When rush hours were so tough
a heart attack might get stepped over
you looked up from the long footpaths
to partings in the houses' iron hair.

Hosts of Depression-time and wartime
hated their failure, which was you.
Widows with no facelift of joy
spat their irons. Shamed by bookishness

you puzzled their downcast sons
who thought you might be a poofter,
so you'd hitchhike home to run wild
again where cows made vaccine

and ancient cows discovered aspirin,
up home, where your father and you
still wore pink from the housework
you taught each other years before ━

and those were the years when farm wives
drove to the coast with milk hands
to gut fish, because government no longer
trusted poor voters on poor lands.

Les Murray

Afterword

Alex McKinnon & Eleanor Gordon-Smith

There we go. All done.

Hopefully you worked your way through the whole thing proper rather than just skipping to the end. If you did you'll still be quietly reeling at the raw talent packed into those 130 pages —gorgeous poetry; spellbinding, haunting artistry; tales of love and horror and ants, the odd typo. We especially enjoyed the contributions from two young starving writers, Mungo and Les. They've got real potential, we think, if they keep working hard at it.

This edition of ARNA comes with a touch of sadness—Robert Hughes, the great art critic, author and general human being, passed away in August aged seventy-four. We won't go into his accomplishments here because afterwords are meant to be short, but if you've never read *The Fatal Shore* or *Things I Didn't Know*, go and find them immediately (after you're done with ARNA, obviously). Hughes contributed to ARNA during his first and only year at Sydney University—in true Arts student style, he was too busy discovering, as he put it, 'beer, girls and university journalism' to attend many lectures or hand in assignments. His academic failure did not stop him becoming one of the greatest Australians who ever lived; indeed, had he diligently pursued his studies instead of tending to the creative spark inside him, we might never have seen Robert Hughes the intellectual giant. We might have had Robert Hughes the barrister instead, as he intended to become when he first enrolled.

You can probably relate to Hughes' time here. It comes as somewhat of a shock to new students when they realise the lecture hall is not the temple of enlightenment it's sold as. A lot of students give up at that point, thinking there's no home for the quiet restlessness that carried them to university in the first place.

A few, though, shrug and write poems and stories and get them published in tiny, dense journals of absolutely no consequence, and when they see their name in print for the first time they go ballistic. They yell and cry and show their mum, and then they sit down and write another one because they've found it, the great glorious thing inside that makes the whole show make sense.

What you've just read represents more than hard work or ambition; everything in this journal was made by people hunting for that feeling. It's the only reason ARNA exists, the only reason anything worthwhile at this university does. We hope some of this year's contributors found it here; most won't go on to be the next Robert Hughes, but we think they've done alright.